George Chittenden was born and bred in Kent, and is the youngest of six children from a working class family. As a child he idolised the character Tintin and spent many summers dreaming of adventures in faraway lands. These days George teaches local history and writes commercial fiction when he isn't backpacking around the globe.

The Boy Who Led Them

"The barbarous hated name of Deal should die or be a term of infamy."

Daniel Defoe

For my ancestors who walked those cobbled streets.

George Chittenden

The Boy Who Led Them

AUSTIN & MACAULEY

A CIP catalogue record for this title is available from the British Library.

ISBN 978 1 84963 128 0

www.austinmacauley.com

First Published (2012)
Austin & Macauley Publishers Ltd.
25 Canada Square
Canary Wharf
London
E14 5LB
Printed & Bound in Great Britain

The Boy Who Led Them

Chapter 1

The English Channel ... 1792

The vessel creaked from somewhere deep within as she left the
crest of another wave and plunged, fully laden with smuggled
goods, into a trough twenty feet deep. A moment later, the
small ship was launched back into the air, knocking every man
but one off his feet and onto the drenched timber of the deck.
The wind whistled through the cutter's sails as the ship
plunged yet again in the sea's vicious cycle. Every man held
on for dear life. Most were paralysed with fear at the fate
awaiting them – all but one.

At the ship's helm stood the notorious smuggler, Jacob
Swift, at twenty-two years old he was a legend in the making.
He stood with his head held up high and his blonde shoulder
length hair blowing in the wind as he battled everything the
English Channel could throw at him.

On this stormy evening though, the weather and rough sea
were the least of his problems. In the ship's wake and giving
chase was a seventy-gun Royal Navy man of war.

The prime minister himself had signed his consent to the
use of whatever resources were needed to eliminate smuggling
on the Kent coast – and Jacob Swift, a man who'd stood up to
his enemies and wielded the power of an army.

Now, as Jacob gripped a telescope with one hand and held
onto the mast with the other, he could only watch as his ship
was forced even further into dangerous waters on a direct
course for the Goodwin Sands, the infamous ship swallower.
Trying to drive him aground on the sandbank was a clever
move on the Navy's part, and one that Jacob himself had used
countless times over the years to escape his enemies.

Once again, he was thrown back and forth as his ship
ducked and dived over the rough water. Jacob glanced around

at the bulk of the war ship visible only a short distance away in the fading daylight and he came to the conclusion that the odds had never been so stacked against him. There was no way out for him this time; that he was sure of. He watched the great ship moving into an attack position. Glancing over at the Kent coast, he could make out the lights of his town not five miles in the distance. It was so frustrating, but then Jacob had an idea that would change the course of history.

Remembering the letter he'd written earlier, Jacob pulled it from his pocket. It was a long shot, he had to admit it, but it was better than nothing. If anyone was going to find the Eye of the Serpent, his men should, it was rightfully theirs. Jacob pulled down a lantern that was attached to the ship's foremast, opened it up, and quickly smothered the parchment in a thin layer of wax to preserve it. Then as he staggered around on deck getting smashed by the rough sea, he found a bottle.

A few minutes later, Jacob struggled to stick the message in the bottle. He jammed the cork down with the handle of his knife and filled it with more wax to seal it. Another wave broke over the deck, and Jacob cursed the day he'd heard about the treasure that had brought him into this situation, and he wondered which of his men had betrayed him.

Suddenly, a sharp whistling sound filled the air – a sound that panicked every man aboard the small ship – but it was too late to do anything now. Jacob looked up to see the man of war illuminated, and he knew exactly what that meant: the gunners were lighting up the cannons.

A moment later, a barrage of cannonballs began raining down on the small cutter, smashing her to bits. Jacob was knocked clear off his feet by the initial impact and hit his head on the deck, knocking him unconscious. As water poured into the vessel from the dozen holes that had been punched through the ship's hull, the message in the bottle, gripped in Jacob Swift's hand, sank along with the ship and the rest of its crew. It drifted down to the bottom of the sea, where it would remain for over two-hundred years, encased in sand, until one day, when that sand would finally shift and deliver that message not into the hands of the legendary smuggler's men but into the hands of a troubled young boy.

Chapter 2

It was six am when the squawking of the seagulls finally forced Stanley awake. As soon as he opened his eyes, that feeling of dread returned, and instantly, he knew that nothing had changed.

"Sleep on it; you'll feel better in the morning," his mother had promised when he'd cried on her shoulder the night before. But now, as Stan climbed out of bed, that gut feeling began aching deep down within him – that dread that came from knowing that he would face the same name calling and sniggering again on Monday morning. Even Stan's so-called friends had joined in on Friday afternoon, not in the name calling but in laughing at Daniel and his friends' insults, at least he thought they did, but maybe that part had all been in his head.

Stan knew deep down that his friends hadn't wanted to do it, but with Daniel's gang, if you weren't with them, you were against them, and anyone against them faced the same ridicule as Stan. Nobody wanted that. Stan didn't blame them; if he could have done something to avoid Daniel's wrath he would have done it too. But Daniel Ryan needed a target for his insults, and only Stan was left to fill the vacancy. So, for the last few weeks at school, and even outside of school now, Stan's life had been hell.

Daniel Ryan had covered everything; he hadn't left a single aspect of Stan's life alone. 'Your dad left you and your mum cos you're skanks'; 'Your mum can't even afford a real house'; and 'You don't wash' were among Daniel's current slogans.

Stan opened the curtains and flooded his small bedroom with the morning light radiating from the sun that was just starting to rise in the blue sky. It was Saturday morning, and it looked like it was going to be a fantastic day. But the dread in the pit of Stan's stomach made him fear that it would all be ruined. Sighing, he decided he was going to try and make the most of the weekend and drag it out as much as he could. Stan decided to try to forget all about Daniel and his gang, at least until Sunday night, and he began getting dressed.

For now, Stan was going to seize the day, so after making some sandwiches and a bottle of squash, he crept into his mother's room. She was still fast asleep, of course, but as he began to gently shake her, she soon awoke and sat up smiling at her son.

"Mum, I'm going to pop out on my BMX," he whispered.

"Sure, darling. Give me a hug," she requested, and as he hugged her, she asked him how he was feeling. He told her that he was feeling much better, which was a lie, but he knew that when he was unhappy, so was she, and this made him angrier at Daniel than anything else. After kissing his mother goodbye, Stan left the house, climbed on his BMX, and rode off towards the sea.

Chapter 3

It was still early enough that Saturday. The small town's streets were virtually empty. Stanley peddled and peddled relentlessly through what was now known as Middle Street, a narrow winding street with branches coming off toward the beach and down toward the High Street. Every house Stan passed dated back centuries and appeared completely unique. He turned off towards the sea and finally emerged on the seafront, where he pulled up next to a bench and sat down, puffing and panting in an attempt to catch his breath.

A thick mist was just beginning to lift over the calm sea, spookily obscuring the end of the pier completely. All that was left was the walkway which disappeared into the unknown. As Stan stared into nothingness, occasionally he caught a passing glimpse of the café and the piers decks where men would pass their days waiting for that dream catch which they'd brag about forever.

Stan inhaled a lungful of sea air and sighed. The sea always seemed to have a calming effect on him; its sheer vastness inspired a feeling of insignificance, which was a feeling that Stan liked. Slowly rotating his head from left to right, he took in the sights of the small fishing town as the seagulls squawked and swooped down from the air, landing elegantly on the promenade where they stared out at the ocean.

The small town dated back hundreds of years and was rich in history, as the houses along the seafront suggested. Other parts of the town were more modern, dating back to the early twentieth century, when the opening of a coal mining pit in the area had created the demand for a huge workforce, and the town's population had rapidly grown. Housing developments had sprung up, almost doubling the number of inhabitants.

Stan lived near the old part, which was good, even though the flat above the newsagent's that he and his mum rented was like a shoebox. Middle Street, the labyrinth of narrow crisscrossing streets, back in the olden days (his mum would always tell him), was the main high street and a hive of activity.

Whilst Stan watched the mist slowly lifting off the ocean, he tried to imagine what the town would have been like. In his mind, he pictured taverns and streets bustling with fishermen, smugglers, and men of the law. Stan smiled to himself at the image in his mind, but he was quickly pulled back to reality by the real image in front of him.

The mist was lifting, swirling, and disappearing into the atmosphere to reveal the concrete pier in all its glory, jetting out into the calm sea. Beyond the pier out in the English Channel, Stan could make out at least a dozen boats of various shapes and sizes. He thought about the Goodwin Sands hidden out there under the sea – a huge sandbank that had claimed hundreds of boats and thousands of lives over the years. On the very horizon, as far as the eye could see, the coast of France loomed in the distance across the water.

As Stan took it all in, he was distracted by one seagull squawking aggressively at another. He focused on the birds and suddenly noticed something else which he was immediately surprised he hadn't spotted before.

The shoreline had been battered by a storm several days before, and the shingle had been shifted so savagely, it appeared as though half the beach had been washed away. It was littered with the usual artefacts and debris: driftwood, old fishing tackle and cuttlefish. But then, something strange caught Stan's eye – something that didn't quite belong – and before Stan knew it, he was sprinting down the beach toward it.

Chapter 4

Stan staggered down the sharp bank where the storm had pushed the shingle violently up the shore, digging in his heels to prevent himself from falling forward. Despite his efforts, the pebbles gave way under his feet, causing him to slide down the bank with an avalanche of small stones cascading behind him. Finally reaching level ground, he ignored the lapping of the calm sea on the shore and tried to regain his bearings.

The glinting of that strange object that only a moment ago had seemed to be drawing him to it had now vanished, but Stan continued his search. For a moment, he scanned the beach which was covered with a wide range of junk stirred up by the storm. Old driftwood that the sea had worn away into smooth and unusual shapes was scattered here and there, joined by cuttlefish and starfish that the storm had forced from the ocean. Staring up the beach, Stan watched as the seagulls swooped and landed on the pebbles, screeching to alert their fellow scavengers of this rare delicacy. Coke cans, bottles and carrier bags were also littered about, but none of this was what had grabbed Stan's attention.

Desperately, he searched, hoping his mind hadn't played a trick on him. And then he saw the unusual glint of the reflection of the morning sun. It was half a dozen metres down the beach, and as he approached it, he discovered that it was made of glass, as he'd suspected. But this glass was unlike any he'd seen before; it was cloudy white and looked half an inch thick.

Stan bent down next to the object and saw that it was actually a bottle, and a strange one at that. It was buried almost completely in the shingle with only an inch or two protruding from the top.

Stan wasted no time in prizing the bottle from the grip the beach had on it, and he held the strange object in his hands for a moment. He was surprised not only by its weight but by its odd shape as well. The bottom was curved rather than flat, and it looked like it had been molded by a blind man. The most unusual feature was the rotten, unusually long cork that was jammed far down the bottleneck.

What surprised Stan the most, though, was that something was still rattling around inside of it. Whatever it was, Stan knew that it was old. His mind began to race with the possibilities. Within seconds, his curiosity escalated and became too much for him to handle. Stan threw the bottle onto the stones and it smashed into pieces, releasing the roll of fabric that had been tucked away inside. Stan carefully picked away some of the shards of glass and scooped up the parchment. It had a strange texture and an unusual smell.

As he unrolled it, he noticed that it was covered in a strange wax, but it was definitely made of some type of fabric. As he opened it up, he caught the first glimpse of it in all its glory. Speechless, he stood listening to his heart beating inside his chest.

The material had strange writing on it that didn't resemble what he had learnt at school, but it was definitely English. After a moment he read the words aloud.

To any of the gang

Were I a man of the cloth, I'd pray this message reaches shore and is retrieved as successfully as the cargoes we've ferried over these troubled years.

Great peril is upon me, and this time, I fear there is no escape. After outpacing their clippers for so long, I thought they'd never catch me, but the time has finally come, and I feel that death is certain. If by chance this message finds you, and you hear news of my demise, buried deep down inside my one true love, you will find a treasure of enormous wealth, a treasure known as The Eye of the Serpent. Good luck, my brothers.

Swifty

Stan carefully rolled up the note and placed it inside a side pocket on his bag with a few pieces of the glass. He struggled to climb back up the steep hill of pebbles, and when he reached the top, he jumped on his BMX and peddled frantically toward where he hoped all the answers to his questions lay: the town's maritime museum.

Chapter 5

Stan zigzagged through shortcuts and back alleys, bunny hopping up and down curbs, racing his BMX all the way until screeching to a halt outside the museum.

It was a small building near a church in the centre of town. Had it not been for the bronze plaque screwed onto the brickwork near the main door, it could have easily been mistaken for a house.

Stan padlocked his bike to a lamppost and entered the building for the first time. Inside, he was surprised. The exterior of the museum was deceptive; the building reached further back than he'd imagined. The building was jam packed with odd exhibits and dozens of glass cases filled with ships. Some were grand like the Cutty Sark, whilst others were less dazzling lifeboat vessels. There were anchors and old cork lifejackets, cannons and old oak barrels. The walls were covered with photos and paintings of old lifeboat men smoking their pipes and savage storms out at sea.

Stan spent a moment taking it all in. There was no doubt that the answers to his questions lay somewhere inside the museum, but finding them, he realized, was going to be a lot trickier than he'd first imagined.

Stan heard a noise behind him. He swung around to the sight of an equally startled old man.

"Sorry, lad, I didn't mean to make you jump. I didn't think we'd have any visitors this early," the old man said. Stan figured that he was at least seventy, maybe even eighty, and he had a grey beard that was much more impressive than the small tuft of hair that remained on his head. What completed the man's look were the glasses that were precariously balanced on the end of his nose. He stood smiling at Stan. "Is there anything I can help you with?" he asked.

Stan felt a little unsure of what to say, and when he did

finally open his mouth, he felt a little stupid when he asked, "Do you work here?"

"I certainly do, my friend. The name's Reg Cooper and this old museum's been in my family for over eighty years." He paused and studied Stan for a moment. "Have a look around, if you like. I won't charge you."

"Thanks," Stan said as he watched the old man stagger by the aid of his stick around the reception desk, his glasses swinging from side to side on the end of his nose. Stan half-expected them to fly off and clatter to the floor, but they didn't, and when the old man was finally settled on a chair, Stan turned his attention to the innumerable exhibits; he knew it would take him forever to trawl through it all.

Walking slowly back to the reception desk, Reg Cooper looked up from the papers he was reading and at Stan through those glasses. "Yes, lad, is there anything I can help you with?" Reg asked.

For a moment, Stan froze, trying to decide whether he could trust Reg; he quickly decided that he could. "There is, actually. I'm interested in a man named Swifty," Stan stated.

The old man let out a faint gasp. "Swifty," the old man muttered, "That's a name I haven't heard in a long, long time."

"So, you know who he was?" Stan asked Reg, who appeared to be deep in thought, like he was contemplating a serious decision.

Suddenly, he looked over at Stan. "Yeah, I know who he was, and I can honestly say I'm one of very few now who knows the real truth," the old man said.

"What do you mean?" Stan asked the old man, who looked deep in thought once again.

Reg looked up at Stan. "Swifty was many things, my lad, and if you really want to know, I'll tell you all about him, but it may take a while."

Stan clutched his bag, recalling what he had kept in it. "I really need to know," he said.

The old man smiled.

Chapter 6

"Swifty," the old man began, "was, to the people who knew him, a man of honour. He was a hero to the poor and an enemy to the rich. He was a man many people admired and many more feared. He helped and protected his people through the darkest times in this town's history.

"But don't think he was an angel, kiddo, not by a long shot. To his enemies, he was a scoundrel and a very dangerous man, never to be trusted. He wielded the power of an army of men who would have died for him. The customs and soldiers of the crown – the very same soldiers he'd made rich over the years whilst his smuggling empire flourished – hunted him down. It was these soldiers who blackened his name with horrific rumours and turned him into the monster that is now depicted in history."

"So, why was he being hunted?" Stan blurted out, unable to help himself.

Reg looked at Stan through his milk bottle glasses and chuckled at his eagerness. Reg himself had been about the same age, and just as keen, as this young man when his mother had told him about the legend of Jacob Swift.

"Patience, my lad," Reg said. "Come take a seat. I've got a feeling it's going to be a long morning." Stan squeezed around the reception desk and sat down on one of the battered old chairs next to the old man and listened patiently as he began to tell the story from the beginning.

"Jacob Swift was born around 1770 on the outskirts of town. He had blonde hair, pale skin and eyes the colour of the sky on a summer's day. His mother died during labour – something he'd always blame himself for. Back then, as you can imagine, the town was a lot smaller. It was a rough place where sailors spent a few days on dry land boozing in the town's many taverns. Crime was rife, especially smuggling, although, nothing like the levels that Swifty's gang would reach in the years to come, but it was happening all the same. It was an exciting place for a young boy like Jacob.

"He was raised by his father, who was a fisherman and a good man – a man who knew right from wrong and who taught his son many things."

The old man paused and looked at Stan. "Lad, there are many lessons in life you can't learn from books. You understand?" he asked, waiting for Stan to nod in agreement before he continued with the story.

"Well, young Jacob, just like you, it seems, was a good listener. He spent most of his childhood out in The Channel with his father on the many different ships his father worked on. Jacob would help his father with his work and he would teach Jacob everything he knew, but, most importantly, he taught him about The Channel and its many deadly sandbanks that often claimed lives. It was this knowledge of the Kent coast that in the years to come would save Jacob's skin on many an occasion.

"Jacob was a brave boy; few things ever scared him, and the ocean, however rough, was never one of these things. He was tough too, real tough. When he reached his teenage years, his father managed to secure him a place in a local school by using his connections with a rich merchant who, among other things, owned a fleet of fishing boats that Jacob's father worked on.

"Back then, schooling was unheard of for people of Jacob's social class, so it was a fantastic opportunity for him, and his father was over the moon. Raising his son to make something of his life had been his wife's dying wish.

"Jacob, on the other hand, had different ideas. He'd already fallen in love with the ocean, and that was where he saw his future. So, leaving his dad during the day and attending a school was a challenge for him, but he made a strong effort for the sake of his father, whom he loved more than anyone.

"It wasn't meant to be, though. After a few weeks, he was thrown out of school for sticking up for a boy in his class. The

27

boy's name was Jim Robson, and like Jacob, he didn't come from rich stock like the rest of the pupils. Jim Robson was overweight and had what people often refer to as 'puppy fat'. In the years to come, he would fill out into a statue of a man, but back then, he looked tubby and would bear the wrath of all the rich kids' jokes for it.

"Not Jacob's, though. He saw bullies for what they were, weak."

With this, Stan's ears perked up. There were a million things he wanted to say to the old man – things that had been building up inside him for weeks while Daniel Ryan and his gang had been making his school life absolute hell. Stan felt like he was going to explode, but he felt strangely comfortable in the company of this old man, who was a complete stranger and yet someone Stan already knew he could confide in.

Stan decided he would be patient and wait. He knew the right time would come. Right now, he needed to know about Swifty, the man who had delivered him the strange message from beyond the grave.

"Jacob," the old man continued, "who spent his lessons at the back of the class quietly daydreaming about adventures out on the open sea, quickly turned his attention to the bullies. He was sharp-tongued, smart, and a loner at heart. Even at that age, he didn't need anyone else. I think he saw it as a way out, like a path leading to his destiny, but that's just my opinion," Reg said.

"Well, soon, the rich kids' jokes were diverted from the tubby kid to Jacob, the rough and ready fisherman's son. Never one to take insults, Jacob lost his temper within a few days and punched one of the bullies. He was thrown out of school, much to his father's despair, and returned to work on the fishing boats, where he spent the next few days working in silence, repairing nets and fearing his father's disappointment.

"But of course, back at the school, with Jacob out of the picture and nobody left to protect tubby Jim Robson, the insults started again. And now that the bullies had been humiliated by Jacob, they were even harsher to Jim.

"Jim Robson, however, had watched Jacob's example with

envy and quickly decided to follow in his footsteps. Just like Jacob, Jim was expelled, and a few days later, the pair came face-to-face near the fish market, where Jacob was delivering his father's catch of the day. Jim helped Jacob carry the empty baskets back up to the beach and load them back onto the boats. From that day, the pair would share a bond of loyalty and trust that would last a lifetime. They'd stick together and watch each other's backs through thick and thin in the troubled years to come, through scrapes with the law and battles on land and sea until the very end.

"To begin with, though, Jacob had managed to secure his new friend a job on the fishing boat that he and his father worked on, the pay was meagre. In those days, it was a struggle to even get by. The work was hard and the days were long, but neither of the boys regretted getting themselves thrown out of school. Jacob would never have dared admitting this to his father, though, who eventually forgave him. Jacob felt bad; he knew his father had wanted him to make something of his life and be more than just another fisherman.

"Well, I guess fate is fate, because Jacob's father got his wish in the end, but had to pay a price for it.

"Months after the pair were thrown out of school, Jacob's father fell ill with a bad case of pneumonia that nearly killed him. It was weeks before he recovered, and even then, he was unable to return to work. The illness had damaged his lungs, leaving him wheezing and gasping for breath after the slightest bit of physical exertion.

"Jacob and his father were suddenly in trouble; neither could survive on the salary Jacob alone received, especially with the mounting medical treatments his father required. Jacob was scared and didn't know which way to turn, but destiny has a way of solving life's problems, and one evening when Jacob was sitting up on the beach watching the ships out in the channel, the solution to his problems found him.

"The sky was darkening over the choppy ocean and the wind was blowing northeasterly when he first witnessed a smuggling boat unloading its contraband – an operation young Jacob would oversee thousands of times in the years to come.

"It all began with a strange combination of flashing signals that caught Jacob's eye. They were coming from a patch of scrub up the coast a few dozen yards and going out into The Channel. Then as Jacob sat there with the wind gusting in his face, he noticed a small vessel out in The Channel flashing back a similar signal, and before long, Jacob was watching a small row boat loaded to the hilt with barrels and crates cruising rapidly toward the coast where he was sitting.

"Within moments, the boat was near the shore. Jacob was fascinated by the strange events taking place right before his eyes, but he was startled by the sound of footsteps behind him. When he turned around, he froze in horror at the sight of a dozen of the toughest looking men he'd ever seen emerging from the bushes on the shoreline.

"One of the men marched straight over to where Jacob sat. He was old and wiry with weather-beaten skin and dark piercing eyes. Jacob recognized him instantly; his name was Billy Bates, the leader of the biggest smuggling gang in the area, and he had a vicious reputation. A moment later, the others joined him, armed with pick axe handles, and they crowded around Jacob menacingly. They were a lot younger and much bigger than the old man, but it was the old man who scared Jacob the most. He stared down at him through those dark eyes of his while Jacob braced himself for a boot in the ribs that thankfully never came.

"Finally the old man spoke. 'You're Swifty's lad, aren't yar?' he asked in a hoarse voice. Jacob was taken aback for a moment. He'd never imagined his father would know such rogues.

"'Yeah, my name's Jacob Swift,' he replied. The old man nodded, looking deep in thought.

"'I heard your father's fallen ill. I'm sorry to hear it. He's a good man – one of the best – and he knows that ocean.' The old man paused, looking out at The Channel and the row boat that had almost reached the shore. 'Second to none,' he muttered under his breath.

"He glanced down at Jacob. 'Do you want to earn yourself some money, boy?' he demanded. Jacob took only a second to reply, and you can guess what his answer was.

"That night, he helped the gang unload the small row boat of its goods and transport them to an old barn on the outskirts of town while keeping a good eye out for any riding customs officers. Jacob found all of it rather exciting.

That night, Jacob proved his worth to Bates, who saw him as a capable young lad, with knowledge of the ocean rivalling his best men, and someone with huge potential. Bates knew that Jacob and his dad were struggling to make ends meet, so he offered him a helping hand, and within a few days, Jacob left the fishing fleet and went to work for Bates, who took him under his wing and began his apprenticeship in the smuggling trade. Jacob immediately recruited the only person he could trust to watch his back, Jim Robson, and the pair went to work."

Chapter 7

"Jacob and Jim started off at the bottom rung of the ladder in Bates' operation. Like all of the rest whose livelihood depended on Billy Bates, they had to earn respect and trust. It was obvious from the start that Bates favoured Jacob and saw a high position for him in his empire in the future, but he made it clear that Jacob would have to earn it.

"Back in the 1780s, smuggling was still fairly straightforward; it was known as the free trade, though it was still illegal and virtually impossible to govern. Preventative measures did exist, but the few riding officers that patrolled up and down our coast were so overworked that it was easy to track their movements and land a cargo openly on the beach, miles from where they were positioned at that moment. The riding officers' pay was low too, making them open to bribery, but Bates considered this a last resort. When the contraband hit the beach, the entire cargo would be loaded onto packhorses and carts within minutes and ferried off to a safe hiding place.

"Back in those days, the profit margins were fairly good too; a 4-gallon tub of brandy could be bought in France for £1 and sold in England for £4. Other cargo like tea offered an even greater profit with 1 pound costing 3 pence to buy on the continent and fetching 25 pence in England.

"The smugglers and working class alike shared the opinion that men like Billy Bates were doing everybody a favour by allowing the poor to access life's luxuries at affordable prices. Believe it or not, back then, smugglers weren't thought of as criminals; all they were doing was cutting out the middle man and supplying goods at a cheaper price. Their actions were even considered noble and heroic by many.

"Jacob and Jim began their careers as tub carriers. A tub was a wooden cask that held about 18 litres of liquor, sometimes whisky or gin, but usually brandy. When a boat would hit a safe spot on shore under the direction of a lander, whose job it was to coordinate the landing, the tub carriers would load up the cargo, stringing several barrels over their shoulders that were harnessed together with rope. They'd also load up the packhorses and carts. This entire operation was carried out swiftly, and within a few moments, the row boat would be paddling back out to sea, emptied of its goods, while a dozen men like Jacob and Jim would load up to the hilt with liquor, tea, and tobacco and make their way to a secure location where the goods could be unloaded and stored overnight.

"While en route, the convoy would be guarded by a handful of batmen – tough guys wielding bats and pick axe handles, who were constantly ready for surprise attacks from either rival gangs or revenue officers. Whatever the case, the batmen were more than willing to ruthlessly use any force necessary to get Billy Bates' cargo to its destination.

"Bates himself had several teams operating independently, and he was very selective when it came to organizing them. If you worked for Bates, you had to understand and respect the chain of command first and foremost. The landers were in charge of the teams and they only took orders from Bates. If you failed to carry out an order from your lander, you were out of Bates' operation, plain and simple. Many of the landers had started out as tub men and had worked their way up over the years, earning Billy Bates' trust and respect every step of the way. Not everyone had what it took to be a lander; you had to possess perfect knowledge of the coastline and the local area, the signalling procedures, and most importantly, the natural ability to use your initiative and think on your feet. The profits in smuggling were high enough to afford to lose a cargo from time to time, but when that happened, the blame always fell on the lander because he was responsible for getting the goods from the boats to the safe houses.

"Billy Bates was a reasonable man, but when things went wrong, he demanded an explanation. The batmen were an important part of the operation. They were usually local tough men who had proven their worth to Bates. Bates would often move his batmen from team to team, always insuring that at least one of his most trusted men was present on every landing. Most of the time, the batmen had it easy; they only worked for their money when things went wrong, and if and when that happened, they would use the bats they carried to fight to the death to protect Billy Bates' cargo.

"Bates himself led a hectic life and was constantly on the move between Canterbury, where much of the cargo was sold and the local towns, where he was constantly conducting business with farmers and landowners to secure the use of cattle for the runs and safe houses in which to secure the goods. He also spent a lot of his time out at sea, and, of course, on the continent where he purchased his goods. He struck deals day and night to secure a steady flow of goods and wages for his workers.

"Jacob had cherished the feeling he experienced during the landings from the very start; not just the excitement from the risk he was taking but the knowledge that he was part of something, having people looking out for you, and watching your back. He felt that, by being part of Bates' gang, he was no longer the loner he'd been for most of his youth. Jacob also found that he had much more time on his hands now that he was neither a fisherman nor a scholar. His days were mostly free, and he understood why they called smugglers 'gentlemen of the night'. He would often wake around midday, after a late night, and spend several hours tending to his father, who had never sat still for longer than five minutes in his entire life and was finding his forced retirement a torture.

"Jacob's father didn't exactly approve of his son's new career choice, and he had warned him against it from the beginning, but he understood that his inability to work was causing a problem and Jacob was doing everything he could to make his father's life as comfortable as possible during these troubled times. Deep down, he felt proud that his son would go to such lengths and take such risks on his behalf, but he never dared to share these sentiments with his son. Surprisingly for Jacob, his father didn't speak too badly of the notorious rogue, Billy Bates. In fact, Jacob was shocked to learn that the pair had grown up together. Both were the sons of fishermen, and, as children, their lives had followed the same path: both were fascinated by the ocean from a young age, just like Jacob was now, but when the boys became teenagers, destiny or greed had forced them in different directions. Billy Bates succumbed to the temptation of far easier money.

"Jacob had been working as a tub man for more than two weeks and was earning twice what he had earned by fishing. He'd even managed to procure a small amount of brandy for his father as well, however, purely on medical grounds. Then, one morning, Billy Bates turned up out of the blue on Jacob's doorstep. As was always the case, Bates was followed by several tough looking men – the bodyguards who escorted him everywhere. As soon as Jacob opened the door, his heart skipped a beat. Bates was the last person in the world he'd expected to see at his door. In fact, Jacob hadn't thought that Bates even knew where he lived, but that was a lesson he'd soon come to learn about the old man with eyes like marbles – a lesson that Billy Bates would drum into him a hundred times over the coming years. Knowledge was power, and Billy Bates seemed to know everything about every person who entered his life.

"For a moment, Jacob just stood there, startled at the sight of Bates leaning against his doorway with a wicked grin on his weather-beaten face. When Jacob invited him in, Bates strolled inside the small shack, leaving his bodyguards outside to guard the door. Bates seemed to scan every nook and cranny with those dark eyes of his, like a reptile, before turning to Jacob. 'Is your father about, Jacob?' he asked, gripping Jacob's shoulders firmly and looking deep into his eyes.

"Jacob knew that the man in front of him was never easily deceived. Nervously, he called for his father, who was resting in an adjoining room, and a moment later, he hobbled through the door. He was wheezing, and this troubled Jacob. Even the slightest physical exertion like getting up and walking half a dozen steps tired him now.

"When Jacob's father looked up and his eyes met those of Billy Bates for the first time in many years, fear washed through Jacob, and in that moment, he regretted everything: getting kicked out of school, but more than anything, agreeing to work for Billy Bates, a man who, according to local rumours, had killed on more than one occasion. Jacob had heard all the horror stories about the sailors the old man had knifed, and now, because of Jacob, he was stood here in his family home.

"Jacob knew that it would have been a wise decision to abandon Billy Bates, but deep down, he had a burning desire to make something of himself and he believed that it was the men who took risks who received the rewards in this life. But in that moment of dread – a moment that seemed to last an eternity – he saw a look on his father's face that he'd never seen before. The two old friends marched toward each other and embraced warmly. Then, Jacob's father looked at his son and asked him to take a walk. Jacob glanced at Billy Bates and couldn't help but notice the old man nodding in agreement.

"Jacob felt left out and slightly angry, but he concealed these feelings as he strolled out of his house. He spent several hours walking along the beach all the way up to Sandwich Bay, gathering his thoughts and staring out at the vessels in The Channel. When he finally returned home, Billy Bates and his bodyguards had left.

"Jacob's father never told his son what the two men had spoken about. Maybe he'd finally realized that his childhood friend had chosen the better path all those years ago. What Jacob did know was that from that day on, his life changed dramatically, and he would always remember that day as the one that marked the beginning of his journey on the path toward his destiny to become the most notorious smuggler in this town's history."

Chapter 8

"Very early the next morning, as the sun began to make its appearance on the horizon, young Jacob Swift was awoken suddenly by a sight that sent shivers down his spine and made him grab the candlestick next to his bed.

"Standing in the doorway of his room was Alfred Bicks, a part-time batman and personal bodyguard to Billy Bates. As the years passed, Jacob and Alfred would grow to be like brothers, but on that morning, all Jacob knew about the man in front of him was what he'd heard, and that wasn't reassuring to Jacob when he opened his eyes to see Alfie grinning down at him. Alfred Bicks was the tallest man Jacob had ever seen at six feet, seven inches. He was skinny and had a long brown ponytail and a bushy beard that hung loosely down to his chest. People said that Alfie was a lunatic and completely unpredictable. Nobody was safe from his savage attacks with the cutthroat razor he always carried.

When Jacob got to know Alfie, he came to understand why the man had such a horrific reputation around town, and, like most things, Bates was responsible. He knew that fear was a powerful tool that more often than not encouraged people to cooperate with requests they'd ordinarily refuse. Bates had cultivated Alfie Bicks' reputation for years by spreading horrible rumours about him. It benefited him tremendously to have some loose cannons at his side, as he put it. Don't get me wrong; Alfie Bicks did carry a razor, and when it came to the crunch, he was more than willing to use it. There were many men in the vicinity who bore the scars to prove it.

"That morning, as Jacob grabbed the candlestick and leapt out of bed, ready to do battle, Alfie Bicks roared with laughter. A moment later, after Jacob understood that he was safe, he joined the big man. When Bicks finally got control of himself, he informed Jacob that Bates had requested his company.

Jacob dressed and the pair rode on horseback through the bustling streets. Along the way, as they trotted past the locals, Jacob gauged the reaction on their faces as they recognized that they were in the presence of the notorious Alfie Bicks. Jacob saw fear in their eyes as they scampered out of the horse's path.

"When they reached the border of the town, the horse began to pick up speed, galloping past Deal castle and all the way up to Kingsdown, which was a few miles outside of town. Finally, they reached a huge house perched high on the chalk cliffs overlooking the sea.

"Outside the house, half a dozen men stood smoking tobacco. They were all top men in Bates' empire. Jacob recognized several of them from some of the landings he'd carried out during the previous weeks.

"As he approached the house, Jacob was surprised by the warm greeting he received. The men shook his hand and patted him on the back as he made his way through the crowd toward the front door. Before that morning, nobody had really paid any attention to Jacob; he'd been just another young ruffian carrying some of the merchandise. When he entered the house, he felt important for the first time in his life; for once, he felt he was more than just a poor fisherman's son. He felt like he was part of something much bigger; it was a feeling that Jacob Swift loved instantly.

"He was led by Alfie through a maze of corridors straight into a large study. The walls were covered with bookcases that were crammed full; Jacob had never seen so many books and had never realized that Bates was such an educated man. Various large maps of the county and the English Channel took up whatever spare wall space there was.

"In the centre of the room stood a huge round table, large enough to seat a dozen men; this too was littered with maps, parchments, and books. Several bay windows overlooked the ocean, giving a perfect view of the beach that stretched far into the distance. Jacob could just make out the wooden pier near where he lived, jetting out into the sea.

"Turning around, Jacob noticed that Alfie had disappeared

after leading him into the room and he was on his own. He felt a little uneasy, but the feeling soon vanished as he began to study a map of the local area. The map had been hand drawn and was surprisingly detailed and remarkably accurate. It was the first time Jacob had seen anything like it. He traced the coast north to Sandwich Bay, eventually reaching the mouth of the River Stour. He then followed the river inland to the town of Sandwich and all the way to the city of Canterbury. Studying the city gave him a rush of excitement. He'd wanted to visit it since he was very young. His father had told him about the beautiful cathedral there with its dazzling towers and had promised to take him one day; it was one of the few promises that his father would be unable to fulfil now that he was unwell.

"Jacob was startled by a recognizable gruff voice that snapped him out of his thoughts. 'Good morning, Jacob,' said Billy Bates, 'I see you like the maps.' Jacob turned around to face him and was instantly taken aback. The notorious smuggler stood in the doorway to the study immaculately dressed in a white cotton shirt and black waistcoat, a gold pocket watch dangling on a chain from one of his pockets, and his black scraggly hair combed back in a ponytail. This sight was a stark contrast from that of the scruffy rogue he'd met on the beach, and if it hadn't been for those piercing dark eyes, he'd have thought it was a different person. Billy Bates strolled over to the window and stared out at the sea.

"'I've never seen a map like this, Mr. Bates, it's so detailed,' Jacob replied.

"He turned to Jacob and smiled broadly. 'From now on, you call me Bill, okay,' he said.

"'Yes, Sir,' Jacob replied, smiling.

"Bates laughed. 'And never Sir. I work for a living, okay,' he said.

"'Okay,' Jacob replied.

"That morning Bill talked to Jacob for hours. Bates was eager to find out what the young man wanted out of his life, what his dreams were, and how determined he was to achieve them.

Bates was far from disappointed about what he learned from Jacob that morning; he could see a lot of himself in the young man. As Jacob poured his heart out about all his dreams and aspirations, Billy Bates revisited his younger days when he'd begun to carve out a name for himself in the town. Billy Bates had been so successful a smuggler because he'd always possessed an almost supernatural ability to judge people. What he saw in Jacob was an unusual combination that Bates had rarely seen in his life.

"Bates saw young Jacob Swift as one of the quiet ones. He was polite and well-mannered; his mind was always at work analyzing situations; he wasn't rash and would always think before making a decision. People like Jacob were rare; they were immune to anger and would never lash out and let their temper get the better of them. Bates could see that spark burning in the back of Jacob's eyes, though, and he knew that the boy was more than capable; above anything, Billy Bates knew that morning that he'd finally found his successor.

"Bates wasn't young any more, and a few years before, he'd realized that when he died, all the things he'd struggled to achieve would have been for nothing. Bates had come to the conclusion that all of the possible candidates were unsuitable; they were too thuggish, and if handed the power that Bates wielded, they'd be incapable of keeping their egos in check. The empire that Bates had worked for decades to build would crumble, leaving the hundreds of people who depended on Bates for their income penniless.

"He had almost given up hope until that evening a few weeks ago when he'd marched over the shingle to confront that boy, and that boy had stared back at him defiantly. Now, as Bates sat in his study asking Jacob to show him on a map what he knew about the Goodwin Sands, the infamous ship swallower just off the coast, and Jacob told him about the masts of various shipwrecks that had floundered and when they were visible at both low and high tides, he knew that his old childhood friend who had chosen to tread the safer path in life had taught his son well. Then, when Jacob went on to explain about the different streams that passed in between the sandbanks, offering safe passage, Billy Bates was stunned. He'd met Naval Captains who knew less, and it was local knowledge like this that was priceless to men like Bates, who survived on the fringes of the law. Jacob finished by explaining about the areas of the sands that were constantly shifting, making them unpredictable, and how it was possible to gauge a rough position using the coastline and distinct landmarks.

"Jacob had been learning such things from his father ever since he could remember, and that morning, he unloaded everything he'd ever been taught. Bates could see that navigation came naturally to Jacob. Like his father before him, the ocean was in his blood.

"At around midday, the meeting was interrupted by a knock on the study room door. The man who Bates had permitted to enter the room was of average height with ginger stubble, and he was harbouring a large belly. Jacob estimated the man was in his late thirties. Alfie Bicks, who towered over his colleague, followed him into the study.

"'Good day to you, Bill,' the man said as he strolled over to Bates and the pair shook hands. Jacob glanced at Alfie and he nodded with a smile.

"'Jacob, this is Carp. He lands for me, and for the next couple of weeks, you're going to work with him,' Bates said as Jacob shook the man's hand. 'Carp's been working with me for years. He's one of my best men. He's going to teach you a few things; see if you've got what it takes.' Carp smiled at the compliment his boss had paid him.

"Jacob looked at Bill and clutched his hand. 'Thank you for giving me this opportunity. I promise I won't let you down,' he said.

"'It's okay, lad, I know you won't,' Bates replied, ruffling Jacob's hair. 'It won't be plain sailing though, you've got a lot to learn. You're going to have to know how to track the riding officers' movements and where to land a cargo depending on their location and the weather conditions, how to communicate with my men on land and sea, and how to organize a team depending on what cargo's being landed – liquor, tea, or baccy

– but I think you're a bright lad and you'll pick it up. Alfie here is going to be at your side every step of the way,' Bates said.

"This was all fantastic news for Jacob. He was over the moon, but there was a price to pay; Bates told him that one day, he thought he'd make a great leader, but he'd have to study hard. From this day forth, Bates wanted Jacob to visit the house that served as his headquarters every day, where he'd spend a minimum of four hours studying.

"Bates would teach him to speak French, among other things, and Jacob found this prospect a little daunting. He didn't have the best track record when it came to studying, but when he thought about how great the opportunity being handed to him he agreed to Bates' requests. When he finally left the study that afternoon with Alfie Bicks and Carp, ready for that night's adventure, he felt like he was on top of the world. But one thing was nagging at the back of his mind, and that was the thought of Jim Robson struggling with the tubs on his own, thinking that his pal had abandoned him. Jacob vowed to make life easier for Jim the first chance he got. He thought a lot of his tubby friend, and would have chosen him before anyone else to stand at his side."

Chapter 9

"Though he would experience many similar evenings, it was that first evening supervising the landing of his first load with Carp and Alfie that would remain etched in Jacob's memory and was destined to come back to haunt him in the years to come.

"The weather was pleasant when the trio left Bill's headquarters on foot. The ocean was as flat as a pond and the blue sky was beginning to darken. They were headed to Prosperity Farm on the northern outskirts of town. As they walked, Carp began to explain to Jacob about some of the different men who worked for Bates. Many of them were old timers who could be counted on, but some of the faces were new and had yet to prove their worth.

"Jacob listened intently, absorbing and storing every word that came out of Carp's mouth. Jacob understood how important it was to know as much as he could about these men. After all, knowledge was power, and as what they were doing was illegal, they had to place a lot of trust in each other. As Carp described some of the men who were working on their team that night, Alfie Bicks strolled along next to them with his beard swinging left to right and his great height casting a shadow that dwarfed theirs.

"Prosperity Farm supplied horses and mules to Billy Bates to facilitate the transportation of heavy goods. A farmer named Havelock owned it. He was a decent fellow and was more than happy to help Bates in return for a little tea, tobacco, and the occasional cask of brandy.

"Carp introduced Jacob to Havelock and explained to the farmer that in the future, Jacob might pick up the animals on his own.

"'Young Jacob here has Bill's consent and is to be supplied with whatever he needs,' Carp stated, surprising

Jacob and making him suddenly feel very important.

"'Our Bill knows best,' the farmer replied before greeting Jacob warmly.

"The sun was just setting and the first stars were appearing in the dark blue sky when they reached the farm and collected the animals. By the time they left, it was nearly dark. They picked up three mules and began leading them back along the track toward the town, and, more importantly, the shore. Jacob's mule was light brown and trotted along in a world of its own, not gaining speed. However sharply Jacob pulled on its reins, it would merely glance up at him with its jaw swinging left to right as it chewed. It had a comical yet wise look, as if it knew that they needed it more than it needed them. Its expression seemed to say, 'I'll help, but at my own pace' and Jacob found the animal very amusing.

"Finally, as they reached the border of the town, Carp revealed to Jacob where the meeting place was; it always varied from one night to the next. He explained how many men were going to be there and what tonight's cargo was. It was tea – great sacks of it. Tea had been slowly rising in price over the last few months, and people were seeking out cheaper sources of it; why buy it in the shops when you could pick it up at a fraction of the price elsewhere? So, Billy Bates was finding a rising demand for it.

"Bates had arranged several runs strictly of tea to build up a little hoard of it. Carp explained that this was unusual, and that normally, a load would consist of a variety of goods. Often, it would be cigars, tobacco, silk, lace, watches, jewellery, wines, and an assortment of different liquors.

"'Brandy was always in there somewhere, though,' Carp said, 'Always in demand, you see. The trick of this trade is to only get hold of whatever goods you know you can shift on; you don't ever want to get lumbered with cargo you can't move, and you only want to move stuff you know you can make a good profit on, you understand?' Carp asked.

"Jacob understood, much more even than Carp himself did. Jacob nodded away, taking it all in. Carp was a good teacher; he was patient and treated Jacob as an equal, which was more than some.

"Carp explained that he currently had two of his best men tracking Mr. Smollet, the preventive officer whose job it was to patrol on horseback up and down our coast, watching for any suspicious activity and ready to call in for back-up if needed. Backup came in the form of a handful of troops from the local garrison and would take a while to muster up, so they posed little risk to the successful landing of the goods. What concerned Billy Bates, though, was the recording of incidents in Mr. Smollet's journal, which was bound to be read by Smollet's superiors somewhere along the line and would eventually draw much more attention from the Customs on their local stretch of coastline.

"This was why Bill made sure his men went to great lengths to guarantee that Smollet never saw a thing.

"'Smollet isn't on Bates' payroll, you see,' Carp explained. 'Could be if Bill wanted, though,' he said, and Jacob asked why Bill paid men to watch Smollet when he could just pay Smollet off directly. 'Bill don't trust men of the law whether they're on the payroll or not... men of the cloth neither, come to think of it,' Carp added, chuckling. 'Bill don't want to risk them getting greedy, you see,' he concluded. Jacob understood Bill's logic immediately.

"When they finally approached the meeting point, they were pleased to see that the men were already assembled. They were a mismatched bunch of rogues. They differed significantly in appearance; some were young and some were old, but they all shared the common quality of the eagerness to earn some coins.

"A handful of the men were long timers: reliable men with families to provide for. Jacob assumed, however, that most would be squandering their wages in the local taverns within a few hours, and he wasn't wrong. Jacob recognized several of the men and knew them vaguely from the landings over the previous weeks, but a handful of the faces were unfamiliar. Jacob, slightly nervous, scanned the crowd. After all, he was new to the game, but he was confident his uneasiness didn't show. Jacob was glad to observe one thing: his pal Jim Robson wasn't in the crowd.

"Carp greeted the men and began laying out the evening's plans. They were happy to hear the cargo was tea, which was nice and light. Carp finally got round to introducing Jacob to those men who didn't already know him. He explained that from now on, Jacob would be working alongside himself, arranging the landings. Many of the men struggled to conceal looks of surprise, but congratulated him all the same.

"Jacob was aware of one man eyeballing him, clearly unimpressed by the news. Out of the corner of his eye, Jacob watched him while he greeted some of the other men who patted him on the back and shook his hand. Jacob knew who he was too; his name was Bobby Jenkins, and he'd popped up in conversation earlier in the evening.

"Bobby was in his mid-twenties and already a heavy drinker, which was a quality Bates despised. More often than not, he could be found in the town's taverns causing trouble, news of which would inevitably travel through the grapevine and into Billy Bates' ears. Bobby fraternized with some characters so unsavoury that even Billy Bates refused to employ them. During the walk earlier on, the only time Alfie Bicks had spoken was when Bobby's name had been mentioned, and all the big man had said was, 'I don't trust that one.'

"When Carp told the crowd that from this day forth, if young Jacob gave them an order, they carried it out as if it had come from Billy Bates himself, most of the men nodded silently, understanding Carp's message and the seriousness of it.

"Bobby Jenkins clearly didn't share his colleague's opinion, though, as he muttered under his breath, 'I don't take orders from kids.' He didn't dare announce such a thing loudly, but he said it loud enough for people to hear him, and as soon as those words were out in the open air, Jacob stepped forward toward Bobby, ready for a confrontation. For a split second, he saw the look of surprise on Bobby's face, and Jacob was confident that even though Bobby was a little bigger and at least ten years older, he wouldn't beat him in a fist fight.

"Instantly, though, as he approached Bobby, Jacob felt a pull on his shoulder and was dragged backwards. Alfie Bicks stepped past him, mercilessly letting go of the bat that he held in the palm of his hand and letting it slide through his grip from the concealed place where he stored it up the sleeve of his jacket, until he finally gripped the handle tightly.

"'What did you say?' he demanded as he stepped toward the crowd that parted, leaving Bobby Jenkins standing alone, staring at the floor. A moment passed, as the suspense built up. People were truly petrified of Alfie and thought he wasn't quite right in the head, but Jacob was already seeing most of it as an act. Alfie was violent, but he was also pretty clever. 'Well then, tough man,' he roared at Bobby, who suddenly, much to Jacob's surprise, looked up and glared at Alfie through blood-shot eyes.

"It was clear that he'd turned up on a run drunk, which was something Bates didn't tolerate. 'I said I don't take orders from kids,' he slurred, staring defiantly at Alfie.

"In a flash, Alfie Bicks swung his bat. It connected with Bobby's jaw with a loud crack that sent him sprawling on the floor as the crowd let out a collective gasp. Alfie Bicks glanced from the unconscious Bobby lying on his back to the crowd in front of him, instantly silencing them. Alfie's face was stern and his eyes were pure white with pupils like pin pricks. He looked completely insane with his scraggly beard hanging down his chin; there was no doubt about it.

"'Let this be a lesson to anyone who dares to question Billy Bates' judgment,' he roared at the crowd. Most of the men were staring at the floor, but the old timers who knew Alfie well were nodding their agreement at his course of action. A chain is only as strong as its weakest link, and Bobby Jenkins was a liability; the old timers knew that much.

A moment later, Bobby Jenkins began to stir and was soon helped to his feet, where he stood swaying slightly and clutching his face, which had already swelled considerably.

"'You're out, Bob. Get yourself home,' Alfie stated to Bobby, who stood there for a moment glaring at Alfie as blood trickled down his chin from the cut that had formed on his bottom lip. Bob was a dangerous man, Jacob could tell by the glint in his eyes, but he wasn't crazy, and craziness was required to stand up to Alfie Bicks.

"So, eventually, Bobby Jenkins turned around and began to make his way back toward the town and the nearest tavern. But just before he left, he gave Jacob a look that spoke a thousand words, and in that look, he made it clear to Jacob that the pair had unfinished business.

"When Bobby finally drifted off into the distance, the team got down to business. One of Carp's lookouts arrived on horseback, bringing news of Smollet's location. The preventive officer was near the bay of St. Margaret, which was a fair distance south, at least three miles.

"Carp turned to Jacob and winked. 'So, my young friend, where would you suggest we land the cargo?' he deliberately said loudly, letting everyone know that it was Jacob Swift, the fourteen-year-old boy, who was calling the shots.

"Jacob smiled, but didn't hesitate to reply. 'St. Margaret's is a distance away over cliffs and rugged land. Even if Smollet spotted our boat approaching the coast, by the time he galloped here, we'd be long gone, so I say that Sandown's the spot.'

"Carp smiled and leaned in closer. 'Not a bad deduction, Jacob. Bates wasn't wrong about you,' he said before he turned to the crowd and ordered the whole team to move toward Sandown, where the old ruins of the Tudor castle stood just north of the town.

"Everybody sprang into action and made their way to the shore, and, when they got there, Carp showed Jacob a small spout lantern that when lit, produced a spot of light that could be used as a signal. Carp showed Jacob how to ignite it and how to signal to the cutter that was a short distance off shore.

"They landed the cargo of tea that night with no problems, and when everybody had gone their separate ways with some money in their pockets, Carp congratulated Jacob on a successful night's work.

"'Remember, lad, Bates pays us to make decisions, and tonight, you made the right decision; it's that simple,' he said before bidding him goodnight and strolling off, leaving Jacob alone with Alfie.

"As the odd pair began to stroll in the direction of Jacob's house, it didn't take long before Bobby Jenkins' name came up. It was Jacob who raised the subject and Alfie who made Jacob feel a whole lot better about the incident.

"'What happened earlier, Jacob, had little to do with you. He's a loose cannon, Bobby is. Bill's had his eye on him for weeks. You've got to remember that you're lucky to be in the position you've found yourself in. You've got real potential, Jacob, I give you that; you're a clever one, and Bates can see that. But most of the rest of them can't because they're blinded by envy. All they can see is that you've got something they haven't, and they don't like it. The likes of Bobby Jenkins are just pawns to Bill, and that's all they'll ever be. You, my boy, you're already in the back row, and if you play the game right, one day, you could be king,' Alfie said, ruffling Jacob's hair.

"They walked in silence for a moment before Jacob looked up at his lanky friend. 'Thanks, Alfie. It's really good to have you on my side,' he said.

"Alfie Bicks chuckled and stroked his beard. 'Don't worry, kid. I got your back every step of the way,' he said.

"As they arrived outside Jacob's house the pair shook hands before Jacob ventured inside for some much earned rest."

Chapter 10

"The next morning, when Jacob awoke, he lay in bed for a long time contemplating many things as the rain clattered against his bedroom window. He had a lot to think about, and he knew that he had to make certain moves if he was serious about becoming a smuggler. Jacob didn't want to enter the game alone. Bates and Alfie were great, and they offered him loads of support, but what he needed was a companion – a right hand man – and he had no doubt that Jim Robson was the man for the job.

"Since they'd both been expelled from school, the pair had grown very close. They shared a lot in common and both had wild dreams that Jacob Swift knew would one day come true. He felt a pang of guilt for bringing Jim into the game, introducing him to the notorious Billy Bates, and encouraging him to quit his fishing job to become a smuggler. Now, Bates was training Jacob for a management position in his empire and Jim was still struggling with the heavy tubs. Jacob told himself that this kind of thinking was stupid; he hadn't abandoned Jim at all, and his sudden promotion was bound to benefit Jim in the long run. If Jim was a real friend, which Jacob knew he was, then he'd be pleased for him and not envious like the likes of Bobby Jenkins.

"Jacob decided that one of the first things he would do that day before going to Bates' headquarters to meet Alfie and study was to hunt for Jim Robson and have a good talk about their future plans. Another thing that Jacob had to think about was what he was going to do with the considerable sum of money Carp had given him the previous evening. Jacob had never had so much money, and he doubted that his father had either. He knew that in the coming months, there was going to be plenty more of it flowing in his direction too.

"Jacob remained in bed, contemplating what mattered to

him, and it only boiled down to one thing, and that was his father. He'd never even met his mother. She'd died bringing him into the world. Jacob knew that his father had loved her dearly, and he'd taken her away from him. His father had never once blamed him and had dedicated his life to raising his only son. In Bates' words he'd, 'taught him well.' Jacob was aware that he owed everything to his father, and he swore to use the money he earned to make his father's life as comfortable as he possibly could. Jacob didn't know how best to go about this, and decided he'd talk to Bates about it; he knew that Bill thought a lot of his father, even though the two men had been out of each other's lives for years. With all of Bates' connections, he was bound to know someone who could provide some support for his father when Jacob was out of the house.

"Now that he'd worked out the solutions to his problems, Jacob felt a little better, and he finally got around to pulling back his curtains and looking out the window next to his bed. He was disappointed to discover that the sky was grey with thick cloud cover; it had been raining hard through the night and the ground was covered in puddles.

"Jacob crawled out of bed and began to dress, noticing for the first time how old and tattered his clothes were and making a mental note to use some of his newfound wealth to purchase some new ones. Pulling on his thick coat, Jacob checked on his father, who was still sleeping soundly, before he slipped out the door.

"It was a fresh morning and Jacob breathed in the sea air as he made his way toward the local market. Along the way, he was taken by surprise by several people who wished him a good morning and enquired about his father. Jacob found this a little unusual, as these same people normally paid little attention to him, but he was in good spirits shaking hands and generally enjoying the attention.

"When he finally reached the market, the rain was beginning to spit, forcing Jacob to pull his coat tight. He purchased a wide selection of provisions, raising suspicion among the stallholders who were surprised that such a young man could afford to buy such luxuries. Little did Jacob know but it wouldn't be long before these same stallholders would learn of Jacob Swift and begin calling him 'Sir'; eventually, they'd even refuse to accept payment.

"That wet and windy morning, when he returned home, he filled the kitchen cupboards. He knew his father would be pleased; Jacob had never seen them so full. Then he cracked two eggs in a pan and brewed up some of the tea that Carp had generously given him the previous night. His father told him how proud he was when he entered his room and presented him with a hearty breakfast. This made Jacob very happy, and he left the house once more to track down Jim Robson with a spring in his step.

"He roamed the streets for a good hour, strolling first along the whole length of Middle Street past the many taverns that were already open for business. The streets were empty due to the rain that had cleared away the usual crowds. Even the working ladies who always hung around Portabello Court were nowhere to be seen, but Jacob still kept an extra eye out for Bobby Jenkins, just in case, while he searched for his tubby friend.

"Eventually, he found Jim up on the seafront sitting under a shelter near the wooden pier, watching the rain as it lashed down over the sea. As soon as Jim noticed his friend walking toward him along the promenade, his face lit up and he jumped to his feet and rushed over to Jacob.

"'Well, well, well, if it isn't my good pal Jacob Swift. What's going on?' he asked eagerly. 'Everywhere I turn, I hear your name.'

"Jacob sat down on the wet shingle and began to explain the previous day's events to Jim, who sat listening attentively, astonished. Jacob poured his heart out to Jim and told him all about his wild plans for the future and how he was going to make the most of the opportunity he'd been given for the both of them.

"The pair talked excitedly for a long time, speculating about the adventures that lay ahead. Eventually, Jacob turned to his friend and gave him a serious look. 'But Jim, we do need to be patient. We've got a lot to learn, so let's just work hard and not get ahead of ourselves. Agreed?' he asked.

"Jim looked deep in thought for a moment before finally replying, 'Agreed.' And the pair shook hands on it.

"'One day, though,' Jacob said, panoramically pointing at The Channel filled with ships, then the beach, and finally at the houses and taverns that littered the seafront, 'all this will be ours.' He said this with such confidence that Jim Robson didn't doubt him for a second.

"Before Jacob left, they talked briefly about Bobby Jenkins, and even though Alfie had told Jacob not to worry, he still asked Jim to keep his ear to the ground for any information about the drunkard. Jacob wanted to know everything about him including where he lived and which taverns he frequented. Jim promised that he would gather as much information as possible without drawing attention to himself.

"The pair shook hands and Jacob began his walk along the seafront to Kingsdown and Billy Bates' headquarters perched high atop the chalk cliffs. It was a long, cold walk, but it was something that Jacob knew he had to get used to, so he huddled inside his jacket for warmth and just got on with it.

"He walked along the shoreline all the while getting blown by the northeasterly wind and staring out at the choppy sea and the channel filled with dozens of ships dotting the horizon. When he finally reached Bates' headquarters, he was greeted by Thomas, one of Bates' bodyguards, who opened the door that would offer Jacob shelter from the drizzle. Thomas was short, but tough looking with a barrel chest and square jaw. When he walked, he swung his huge shoulders from side to side, and Jacob couldn't help but think that if you hit him with a bat like Alfie had hit Bobby the previous night, Thomas would just laugh before tearing you apart.

"'Well, if it isn't the man of the moment,' Thomas exclaimed, extending one of his shovel hands to shake Jacob's. When Jacob finally managed to retract his hand, which he'd doubted being able to do when it had first disappeared in Thomas' grip, he was led once again into the study, where he got a surprise.

"The large, round table was surrounded by rather unsavoury looking characters who all broke from their apparent meeting and stared at Jacob as he stood awkwardly in the doorway. For a moment, he thought he'd disturbed the group and his presence wasn't welcome. But as soon as Billy Bates set his dark eyes on Jacob, he leapt up from his seat at the head of the table.

"'Jacob Swift,' he roared as he marched around the table toward him, 'the boy who squared up to a drunken Bobby Jenkins last night – his first night on the job.'

"Young Jacob's heart raced as Bates, the man who'd killed numerous times, approached him. He didn't know how to take this; was Bill angry with him? Had he messed up already? But as Jacob glanced from Bates to the table and at the rest of the men who were laughing and nodding, he caught eyes with Alfie Bicks, who winked at him, and he had his answer.

"Bates finally reached out to Jacob, clamping both hands firmly on his neck, and kissed his forehead before telling him in that very distinct croaky old voice that he was proud of him.

"When he let go, he took a step backwards and said with a laugh, 'Alfie here reckons if he hadn't have held you back, you'd have put him down.'

"This caused most of the table to erupt in laughter, but it was in good jest, and it wasn't long before Jacob joined in as well.

"'But remember, lad,' Bates said quite seriously, suddenly silencing the laughter, 'if someone needs to be taught a thing or two, then Alfie here is the one to do the teaching. That's what I pay him for, and believe it or not, he's pretty good at it.'

Everyone's eyes had fallen on Alfie Bicks, who smiled eerily at his boss' compliment while he twisted the end of his beard.

"'You clear on that, Swift?' Bates asked, looking at him straight-faced.

"'Understood,' Jacob said while nodding before Bates roared with laughter once again and beckoned him to take a seat next to him at the meeting of his inner circle and most trusted men, 'the back row' as Alfie Bicks put it."

Chapter 11

When Reg Cooper finally stopped talking he pushed the small glasses he wore that were normally perched precariously on the end of his nose further up towards his eyes and he stared at Stanley waiting for the young man to say something. It took Stan a moment to compose himself whilst he got sucked back to reality.

"I think it's time we had a brew lad, what do you think?" the old man asked shattering the silence.

Stan glanced around at the clock and was amazed to discover that nearly two hours had passed since he'd entered the museum. Where the time had gone exactly he had no idea, he felt like he'd been transported to a different time and place but the one thing he did know was that he wanted to hear more of the story. Stan was grateful that Reg was willing to tell it and he knew he had little choice but to go at the old man's pace so he concluded that he'd have to be patient and wait for a while until the old man was ready to continue.

"Yes, that would be nice," Stan replied, watching as Reg Cooper slowly climbed to his feet and shuffled through towards the backroom.

"Watch the desk for me, lad," he hollered over his shoulder as he disappeared out of sight leaving Stan alone.

Sitting in silence he stared at the exhibits and for the first time Stan saw them in a different light, a moment later he was on his feet sliding around the reception desk and searching for items that he now recognized.

It was only a moment before he came across a pair of small wooden barrels that were strung together with rope. Stan knew exactly what they were and what they were used for. They were tubs that carried smuggled liquor. He pictured Jim Robson with them slung over his shoulders with one barrel on his chest and the other down his back. Stan wondered what liquor they'd stored, he knew they were the real article and had been around in Billy Bates' heyday; he wondered if Jim had ever carried this very pair, Jacob Swift himself even. It was a thought that sent shivers down Stan's spine.

"How many sugars?" he heard Reg shout from the back room, startling him.

"Um two please," he replied before moving on and scanning more of the museum's walls and display cabinets for anything that caught his eye. Stan hadn't taken two steps before he came across a small tin lamp that loosely resembled a watering can. Stan knew what it was immediately, it was a spout lantern and he wondered how many times it had been used to carry signals from ship to shore and vice versa. What cargoes had this small device helped to smuggle into England?

Stan was still holding this thought letting his imagination run wild when Reg Cooper hobbled back into the small museum's main room struggling to carry both cups and support himself with his walking stick simultaneously. Stan quickly rushed over and relieved Reg of the cups. "This place is amazing," he said nodding at all the artefacts.

Reg Cooper's face lit up and he smiled proudly as he looked at Stan through his glasses that had once again made their way south and were perched on the end of his nose. "I think so too," he said thoughtfully looking over at the stacks of strange objects before turning to Stan. "But, unfortunately, few people feel the same as me and you these days, I'm lucky to get a dozen people walking through those doors a week," he said regretfully as he glanced at the empty entrance.

"When I was younger," he continued. "Parents took their kids out for the day to places like this; they had fun and learnt a thing or two in the process. Nowadays kids don't want to go to places like this, not when they see all these theme parks advertised on the telly, it's the harsh reality of business I suppose but people like me can't even compete with kid's attention against competition like that."

Stan took a sip of his tea whilst he tried to think of something to say; he felt genuinely sorry for the old man before him. "So how do you turn a profit and stay open?" he asked finally, causing Reg Cooper to laugh out loud.

When Reg finally got control of himself, he turned to Stan. "In this game there's no such thing as a profit, never has been. This place has been kept running for the last few years on some money that I inherited when my brother passed on, that's what's been paying the electricity bills, but that's dwindling away now and before long it will have gone and when that happens I dread to think what I'll have to do," Reg said sadly.

Stan took another sip of his tea slurping loudly in the silence of the museum; he knew it was a bad habit but he couldn't help it.

"So why do you keep it open?" he asked, he hadn't really wanted to and knew it was a bad thing to ask but it was such an obvious question it seemed unavoidable.

Silence filled the air as Reg Cooper thought hard before replying. "I suppose it's because this place was my parents' dream and they worked hard to make it a reality, and because it's the right thing to do I guess. People these days are so obsessed with money that they've forgotten about what it actually is. You know, Stan, that a wise man once said that if you don't know the past you can never be prepared for the future and I think there's a lot of truth to that." Reg said before silence filled the museum once again as the old man let this sink in.

"I suppose what it comes down to," he continued. "Is that I've got a responsibility, I mean most people aren't that interested in this town's history but, from time to time, a few are and as long as my old heart's still ticking away I plan on being here to show them; what happens when I'm gone is a different story," he concluded.

The old man and the young boy stood in silence sipping their tea for a moment staring at the odd exhibits that Reg Cooper and his family had taken nearly a century to accumulate. Stan was thinking about the message he'd found in the bottle, he was so tempted to show it to Reg whom he knew he could trust, but he resisted the temptation and held back. Stan wanted to know the whole story of Swifty first so finally he broke the silence. "So what happened next?" he asked trying to sound casual and making Reg smile in the process.

"I think it's time we both sat down, like I said earlier it's a long old story and we've only just started," Reg said, and this made Stan smile too. So they both made their way around the reception desk and took up their seats once more as Reg Cooper continued the story where he'd left off.

Chapter 12

"Jacob Swift wasted no time in talking to Bates about his father's medical condition and just as he'd expected Billy Bates came up with the perfect solution. Within days his father had a nurse who visited the house twice a day. She was a nice old lady named Rose who lived locally. She prepared meals, cleaned and generally kept Jacob's father company during the long hours when Jacob himself wasn't around.

"For the next few weeks Jacob spent his days studying at Bates headquarters perched high up on the cliffs, and during the evening he would land cargoes with Carp on the beaches all around the coast.

"Billy Bates proved to be a good teacher; he was patient with Jacob and motivated by the boy's eagerness to learn, and he taught Jacob all about the different ships out in The Channel, the differences in their design, their different uses and whom they belonged to. Jacob found it fascinating, just the thought of the far-off lands beyond the horizon where many of the ships were destined set his imagination on fire.

"Jacob was surprised to learn of the many other smugglers operating on Billy Bates' doorstep, Bates didn't think of them as his rivals either. To him they were his brothers. Many of them were actually good friends of his. Every now and then he'd do them a favour or vice versa, if they were short on numbers and needed to borrow some men to land some goods or needed somewhere safe to stow a cargo Bates was always willing to offer a helping hand.

"When Jacob arrived at Bates' every morning the first thing he would do was study The Channel through Bates brass telescope, scanning the horizon he'd note which ships were still at anchor and which had left and begun their long journeys over to the colonies or to India to purchase silks and other luxuries that Jacob knew would eventually end up passing through his hands when the ships finally returned and anchored up fully loaded.

"One day Jacob arrived at Bates' to discover the old man himself studying The Channel with a look of concern etched on his weathered face. When Jacob asked what was wrong Bates told him to see for himself and when Jacob looked through the telescope he saw a sight for the first time, a sight that in later years would send terror through his bones, a Customs and Excise cutter. It was a fast one too and Jacob could tell by its design that it would easily outrun Bates' ships.

"Jacob knew why his boss had that grave look plastered on his face, thankfully though that evening when they landed a cargo on the beach the cutter was nowhere to be seen on the horizon. But from that day Jacob knew just as Bill did that there was trouble ahead.

"As the weeks turned to months Carp finally gave Bates the thumbs up that The Boy knew everything there was to know when it came to landing goods. Jacob Swift began running a crew of his own and good at it he was, he still had Alfie Bicks and his blood-stained bat close by, but it was The Boy who was the one in charge giving men, twice his age, orders. Before long he established strong bonds with many of Bates' men, especially the younger ones who were fairly new to the game and hadn't been around in Bates' heyday; they felt they had more in common with The Boy as he was often called than they did with the notorious Billy Bates.

"Whilst the months passed, Jacob ventured even further into Bates circle of trust, he was taken to all of the old man's safe houses where cargo was stored both around the town and further inland en route to the city of Canterbury. He was introduced to many of Bates' associates, men of wealth and power that even Bates' most trusted men like Alfie and Thomas hadn't met. Bates even took his protégé over to the continent, to the warehouses in France where most of the goods they smuggled began their long journeys. During the visits Jacob wasn't allowed to speak in his own tongue and Bates was mightily impressed to watch him converse in French with the merchants he'd trade regularly with in the years that lay ahead.

"As time passed by, Billy Bates slowly handed over more and more responsibility to Jacob. Bill wasn't young anymore and he knew it, the long journeys on horseback were too much for him, he was happy to take a backseat and let Jacob manage his empire, though he was still the one pulling the strings and making the decisions.

"In the mornings when Jacob arrived at his house on the cliffs the pair would talk privately and Bill would lay out what needed to be done, Jacob would set out on horseback with Alfie shortly after. He'd visit many people and make endless arrangements on his journeys.

"One morning when Jacob returned home he found his father in tears; he brushed them away as his son entered the room but Jacob knew his father and knew why the man was troubled. He missed being out on the open sea with the squawk of the gulls and the salty air, he'd spent his life out on the rolling waves and now he was virtually housebound it was driving him crazy.

"Jacob took his father out for short walks on the seafront as much as possible. During these walks his father would soon become breathless but it was all worth it for the look on his father's face when he glanced out at the ocean and the warm feeling it gave Jacob deep inside. Jacob knew he had to do something; more than anything he needed his father to be happy.

"A few weeks later Jacob and his father moved out of the small house they'd lived in since Jacob came into the world and into a much larger townhouse on the seafront overlooking The Channel. It was only made possible by Billy Bates who offered his young protégé a sizable loan. By this stage the pair were much more than business partners, they were great friends. Bill had always been wise when it came to money and over the years he'd amassed a small fortune; he had no real family aside from the men he employed and he knew that Jacob would pay back every penny of the loan. Bates saw it as a great investment in Jacob's future and something to focus him, not that he needed it.

"Jacob Swift was a hard worker and never needed to be told twice to do anything, but most of the time Bates found he no longer needed to tell Jacob to do it in the first place and that The Boy was always one step ahead.

"Jacob now sported a fine wardrobe and dressed even better than the rich kids he'd so despised at the school, the difference now though between him and them was that Jacob could venture anywhere in the town, even the rough taverns and areas where stabbings were a regular occurrence, in complete safety. People knew who Jacob Swift was. He was Billy Bates' boy and someone you didn't mess with if you valued your life. When he strolled along Middle Street people greeted him warmly bowing and shaking his hand. The working girls would all swarm around him and squabble over his attention, which always brought a smile to Alfie Bicks' face.

"Life had been changing pretty fast for Jim Robson too and, whilst the months had passed by for him, he'd grown in height and swelled in size, that puppy fat that had earned him the slur 'tubby' and had been the root cause of both Jacob's and Jim's expulsion from the school turned into raw muscle. Jim no longer struggled carrying the tubs. He worked hard and was always keen for a challenge.

"One evening when he was landing a cargo with another of Bates' crews he overheard somebody bad mouthing Jacob. Jim Robson, always the loyal friend, didn't hesitate swinging for the man and flooring him with a barrage of devastating blows. When Billy Bates heard of this incident he called for a very nervous Jim who was expecting the worst when he arrived at Bates' headquarters.

"Bill though shook Jim's hand and complimented him on his loyalty. 'It's a gift you can't put a price on lad.' Bates said as he presented Jim with his first bat.

"Bates figured that tub men were ten a penny and if Jim was so keen to watch his friend's back then who was he to stop him, Billy Bates also knew that Jacob Swift was still a young man, he was earning good money and drawing a lot of attention in the town, one more pair of eyes watching his back wouldn't do him any harm.

"Now with Alfie Bicks and Jim Robson at his side young Jacob Swift went to work; he arranged cargoes with the French merchants and landed them on the town's shores; he kept all the men happy with money in their pockets and kicked back the lion's share of the profits to a very happy Billy Bates who now spent most of his days in semi-retirement at his cliff-top house. Bill had never made such easy money, he advised Jacob on everything before The Boy made a decision but it was always the right decision that he made and, as Jacob switched cargoes, Bill saw a steady increase in profits.

"Everybody was happy and earning good money but the good times couldn't last forever."

Chapter 13

"The trouble began on a pleasant summer's evening only a few weeks later. It came suddenly from nowhere and, until the end of Jacob Swift's days, it never completely went away. Over the years it seemed to attack them in waves, there were times when Jacob felt safer and times when he felt threatened but he was always kept on his toes from one day to the next.

"On the day that it all began, Jacob and Bates had spent a considerable time studying The Channel through Bates' telescope. Like always it was busy with traffic moving to and fro but what concerned the pair was a cutter anchored not a great distance off shore. It flew no flag and carried no distinguishable markings. There was no activity on decks either and this raised Billy Bates' suspicions.

"Eventually, though, Bill sent Jacob off to gather the team for that evening's landing.

"'It probably belongs to a merchant stopping over in the town for a few days, try not to worry lad,' he'd said.

"A cargo was on its way over The Channel and it was too late to do anything about it by then anyway so Jacob set off with Alfie Bicks and Jim to Prosperity Farm to pick up a few mules before meeting the rest of his team at the entrance of Red Brick Lane. Jacob greeted the men warmly. They were in good spirits and eager to get on with the evening's work. The unidentified cutter earlier had unsettled him but it was more than just that. It was like a sixth sense, an instinct young Jacob would come to rely on in the years to come, and an instinct that would save his skin on dozens of occasions.

"That night was the first time he felt it and he knew in his heart that something wasn't quite right. Thankfully, Jacob Swift trusted his instincts that night and he did something that he'd never done before. Taking two extra men aside so the rest of the team would not overhear, he dispatched them on horseback to join his other lookouts and make a complete sweep of the surrounding coastline in both directions.

"'You see anything out of the ordinary you gallop back here, understood? I have a feeling old Smollet isn't our only problem this evening,' he warned them before they galloped off quickly disappearing into the distance allowing Jacob to turn to his team and get on with the task at hand.

"Jacob ordered the team to make their way through the town and up to the shore near the seafront. This alone was out of the ordinary as it wasn't wise to land cargoes in front of prying eyes but Jacob wanted to be near the town in case he needed to beat a quick retreat. If his fears turned out to be unfounded, then all he would have to do was signal to the ship carrying his goods using the spout lantern in his pocket and arrange to meet them further along the coast.

"Marching along through the cobbled streets Jacob felt like a general leading his troops into battle, they were quite a sight and people ran back into their houses and bolted their doors as the gang approached. When they reached the shoreline Jacob squatted on the shingle and pulled out a small brass telescope from his pocket, it was state of the art and had set him back a pretty penny but, at times like this, Jacob knew it was worth its weight in gold.

"Scanning the horizon his eyes passed over dozens of vessels, but Jacob was only searching for one and he quickly realized that the suspicious cutter that had troubled both Bates and Jacob himself earlier in the day was nowhere to be seen. Jacob didn't know whether to feel relieved or troubled by this, but he didn't have time to spare so he quickly scanned The Channel once more and a moment later he'd found his own vessel in the distance making its way towards the coast fully laden with cargo.

"Jacob took several deep breaths to calm himself down. He felt anxious and vulnerable more than anything. He wanted to get the cargo landed and stashed up so he could get his men off the streets. They were attracting far too much attention for The Boy's liking. Jacob knew he would have to be patient for a moment as the ship sailed closer to shore and within signalling range.

"Peering through his telescope once more at the ship, which was now much more visible he noticed that something was amiss. He could make out his men on deck rushing around and it took a moment for Jacob to realize what they were doing, they were unloading barrel after barrel overboard into the sea. Jacob froze whilst his mind tried to figure out what was happening in front of his very eyes. Then, as the vessel swung slightly as it prepared to turn back out to sea it revealed a sight that sent shivers down Jacob's spine and made everything clear. Behind the smuggling ship and giving chase was the suspicious cutter, now though it was no longer at anchor and it was flying the flag of Customs and Excise.

"Jacob's men were unloading the ship in an attempt to lighten the vessel in hope of escape. Whilst all this dawned on Jacob, it was as if time had stopped but then suddenly he heard the gallop of horses' hooves on the cobbles piercing through the summer's night pulling him back to reality. He spun around and faced his men who knew something was wrong, even Alfie and Jim were clutching their bats and staring at him waiting for orders.

"Jacob watched his four lookouts approach on horseback galloping wildly along the cobbled seafront, as soon as they were in ear shot he heard one of them shout, 'Riding officers, a dozen or so armed and on their way.'

"Jacob now had all his suspicions proven. It was an ambush on sea and land. The Boy wasted no more time. All the men were staring at Jacob with panic in their eyes. 'Scatter! Leave the mules!' he roared at the team who quickly began beating a retreat through the labyrinth of streets were they'd no doubt seek refuge in the countless taverns.

"Alfie Bicks rushed over to the horses and mounted one, he galloped the short distance to where Jacob was stood and hauled him up onto the animal. Jim Robson had followed suit. Whilst the horses began to pick up speed Jacob clung on tightly to Alfie as he glanced back at the ocean relieved to see that their ship had unloaded all of its cargo, which was now floating in its wake. The customs vessel had thankfully given up on chasing its prey and had opted for retrieving its rewards instead as men pulled barrels up overboard.

"Suddenly Alfie Bicks cursed and pulled violently on the reins. Turning around Jacob saw what was troubling his friend. They were a fair way back but still giving chase, Jacob could see the red of their uniforms and hear the clatter of hooves. Jacob couldn't help but smile to himself as he was hit with a rush of adrenaline that flowed through his entire body. Alfie turned through the maze of streets and after some sharp turns it appeared like they'd finally lost their pursuers.

"Jacob knew they'd lost the cargo but that was no big deal. The only thing that really mattered was escape. It had been close, way too close."

Chapter 14

"When the riding officers had reached the shore they'd split into two groups and galloped off in different directions. One group gave chase to the smugglers who were on horseback, recognizing them clearly as the leaders. Whilst another group stayed in the town and began searching the many taverns in the surrounding area for the men who'd fled on foot. Many of the locals came out of their houses to see what all the commotion was about having heard the thunder of hooves on the narrow cobbled streets. Others were dragged out from the taverns into the street and searched.

"Meanwhile word of the ambush was spreading through the town like wildfire. At least half the town was employed in the smuggling trade one way or another, the other half bought most of their goods at affordable prices off men like Billy Bates. Nobody was innocent.

"The change in approach by the customs men would have an effect on everybody. That night when the customs men failed to apprehend any smugglers they decided to offer a reward for information.

"'One of you knows something,' an officer shouted at the top of his voice as he marched up and down staring at the crowd who were all silent, even the drunks, returning the officer's gaze with contempt. Everybody present knew it was Billy Bates, the town's most notorious smuggler, they were really after; he hadn't been seen around town for a while and there were even rumours that he'd finally retired and left the boy people called 'Swifty' to run his business. Either way, nobody was willing to offer up any names and it wasn't just the reprisals by Bates' men that kept them silent, though it did help. It was the fact that men like Bates were like their brothers, local people who risked their necks on a daily basis to help them. Billy Bates was one of their own and the men in front of them who were armed with guns and were threatening and harassing them weren't. They were men of the crown and despised for it.

"Silence filled the air for a long moment that made many present feel deeply proud, finally the Customs officer tutted shaking his head before he climbed back onto his horse and began to gallop out of the town with all his men following.

"When the officers were out of sight, the silence was broken with laughter and nattering as most of the crowds began piling back into the taverns to continue their drinking whilst they relived their moment of defiance in the face of authority.

"A handful of men remained outside. They were made up mainly of tub and batmen that worked for Jacob and Bates. Most were low level and just helped out on the odd landing. A few had only just arrived at the pub before being dragged back outside having fled the beach, several others worked alongside Bates' competitors but had a shared interest and were eager to offer their help to the old man with eyes like chunks of coal. The men talked for a few moments and speculated about whether or not The Boy had managed to escape before they decided to dispatch some messengers to inform Bates' top men like Thomas, Carp and a handful of others about the evening's events.

"Only a short time later Billy Bates' back row began to arrive at his headquarters perched high up on the cliffs. Among these men was a shaken Jim Robson; he'd followed Alfie Bicks' example and in the heat of the moment had commandeered a horse which he'd managed to escape on through the skin of his teeth, he'd tried to keep up with Alfie and Jacob but in the midst of chaos had chosen to gallop off in a different direction in an attempt to lead the customs officers away from the pair and improve their chances of escape.

"Billy Bates gripped Jim's hand and leant in closely so that only the young man would hear. He congratulated him on his bravery before adding, 'The Boy was right about you,' in his rough old voice. Billy Bates wasn't too surprised about the night's events, though he was far from pleased. He'd been in the game along time and had been expecting trouble for a while.

"Bates sat Jim down offering him a brandy to calm his nerves before encouraging him to recite the evening's events in as much detail as possible. Bill sat listening intently as he absorbed every last word that his young batman spoke before he asked a number of questions. Billy Bates was more than impressed to hear that his young protégé had sent out more lookouts before arriving at the shore. It was these lookouts that had eventually raised the alarm in the nick of time and saved a dozen good men from certain jail. In Bill's eyes, Jacob had thought on his toes and made the best of a bad situation.

"'But where was he now'? Bill wondered. 'Surely he would have arrived back already?' Bates was relieved that Jacob wasn't alone and was with Alfie Bicks. When it came to the crunch you couldn't ask for a better man at your side, Bates knew this from personal experience. But as the minutes ticked by, concern turned to panic and slowly the old man had to conclude that it was likely the pair had been arrested and detained.

"Eventually Bates was forced to begin the meeting; they had a lot to talk about and many problems to solve. The old man didn't like to press on in The Boy's absence but time was of the essence and he had no choice. Sweeping around the table he wasn't surprised at his men's suggestions.

"'They've declared war on us, Bill, we need to attack them where it hurts and burn out their cutters, lets deliver a message that we're not to be messed with,' Thomas raged.

"'He's right boss, we outnumber them ten to one,' another man chipped in.

"Bates was strolling around his study rubbing his chin deep in thought, listening to his men's opinions, when he suddenly turned and faced the table. 'And you Carp, what do you think we should do?' he asked the man who'd been successfully landing cargoes for well over a decade.

"Carp looked up from the table and into his boss's dark eyes, 'I think we shouldn't be rash Bill, we could make the whole situation a good deal worse.'

"Suddenly the men heard heavy steps up the main staircase breaking up the meeting and causing them to reach for their weapons. Bates braced himself for confrontation as the study's oak door swung open to reveal Jacob Swift red in the face and breathing heavily, he was closely followed by an equally tired-looking Alfie Bicks who had that crazy look in his eyes.

"Crossing himself with his right hand for the first time in many years and muttering, 'Thank the Lord' under his breath, Billy Bates rushed over and greeted the pair.

"It took a while for everybody to calm down enough for the meeting to continue. Alfie recited the story of how the pair had been chased on horseback for miles before they eventually found refuge hiding under the floorboards in an old barn. The pair had laid there in silence for the best part of an hour to be sure they'd lost their pursuers before continuing on their journey.

"Bates and the rest of the men present listened to Alfie's story excitedly and congratulated the pair on a lucky escape before The Boy took over the meeting. Jacob immediately suggested dispatching a rider to the port of Sandwich where their boat was due to dock, they needed to know if their cutter had made it safely back to shore. It was a valuable asset and losing it to the crown would be disastrous. Everyone agreed that it was of the utmost importance and one of the dozen men gathered left immediately to begin the journey.

"The men began debating once again about what course of action to take and it wasn't long before the meeting had descended into chaos, many of the men were keen on revenge and they voiced this opinion. Thomas, squat and tough looking, was always eager for some trouble and was the keenest to stage a counterattack but he was more than aware that, whilst Billy Bates lived, it was he who made the decisions.

"After several minutes Jacob rose to his feet and banged his fist down on the table in anger, silencing the crowd who all looked up at him embarrassed for letting their emotions run away with them.

"'Listen, we don't know nearly enough to make any sort of

decision at the moment,' he stated turning to Bates. 'It was you who taught me knowledge is power and what we need now is just that... information. Before we know it tonight may have been a one off or we may face this much hassle day-in, day-out. We just don't know. So before we do anything I suggest we find out, agreed?' he demanded.

"The men were still silent but were now nodding their agreement, all but Bates who was seated with a smile on his face. Everybody knew The Boy talked sense and, unlike the rest of the men, he hadn't allowed his anger and frustration to affect his ability to make decisions. They all slowly looked up at The Boy and in that single moment every man present understood why Billy Bates had selected Jacob, the fisherman's son, to take over his empire. Not one man at the table had any qualms about taking orders from him.

"They all seemed to mumble 'Agreed' in unison before Jacob turned his attention to Bates who was seated in his chair rubbing his chin with that crooked smile still etched on his weather beaten face.

"'You once told me that you thought old Smollet could be bought, he wasn't there tonight with the rest of them but I guarantee he knows something, I think the time has come to buy some information,' Jacob said.

"Billy Bates nodded. 'You know I was thinking along the same lines' he mumbled before turning his attention to Thomas. 'Take two men and go pay our friend a visit,' he ordered.

"Thomas rose from his chair and glanced at the clock hanging on the wall above the fireplace. 'It's late boss, you think he'll still be awake?' he asked.

"Bates considered this for the briefest of moments. 'If he isn't, it's even better, we'll catch him off guard and unprepared.'

"Thomas nodded agreeing with the old man's logic before he signalled for two of his best men to accompany him and they strolled towards the study door.

"'Thomas,' Bates said getting his bodyguard's attention. 'One last thing, don't hurt him unless it's absolutely necessary, ok.'

"Thomas smiled eerily as he caught a small bag filled with money that Bates had tossed in his direction. A moment later he disappeared with his men out of the room. Now that some action had been taken the men seemed to relax a little; they sipped brandy and speculated about the possible options for their future. An hour passed by slowly before the trundle of hooves on the track outside signalled Thomas's return.

"A moment later the squat bodyguard and enforcer entered the study bringing news. Smollet had given up everything he knew voluntarily; Thomas, for once in his life, hadn't even had to make one threat. Old Smollet, the man who'd patrolled their coast for the last decade, rather unsuccessfully according to his superiors, had been forced into retirement. Thomas explained that Smollet was peeved at this after years of loyal service and was quick to snatch the money from Thomas's hands and give up everything he knew. Unfortunately what he did know wasn't the best of news for the men gathered around the table.

"Smollet hadn't been replaced by a younger more observant officer he'd been replaced by a team half a dozen strong, men who were eager to do away with the smuggling trade for Queen and Country. If this wasn't devastating enough, the suspicious clipper was also destined to be a regular fixture on the horizon from this day forth. The government was fed up with losing out on a fortune in lost revenue from the hoards of taxable goods that were being illegally brought into the country on a daily basis.

"Jacob Swift had wanted information and now he had it, the future wasn't going to be plain sailing from now on, it was going to be a lot harder but The Boy wasn't scared and he didn't mind a challenge. If Customs and Excise were going to change their tactics, then so was he. He didn't quite know how but he knew they would have to adapt to survive."

Chapter 15

"For weeks and weeks it felt like they were fighting an unwinnable war. If the smugglers managed to misdirect the half dozen riding officers on land which was a huge task in itself the customs cutter would more often than not intercept Bates' vessel forcing them to lose all of the cargo overboard, more loads were being lost than were being landed successfully and as a result the profits disappeared. Most nights Jacob Swift found himself paying out his men's wages and operating at a loss; he knew things couldn't go on like this for much longer.

"The Boy met regularly with Smollet who was keen to feed the smugglers with helpful information at a price, but it was beginning to be a price they couldn't afford. The stores of liquor and tobacco that Bates had stashed up quickly began to run dry and with demand for such goods not being met prices began to rise. This in itself wasn't bad news for Jacob who knew that every smuggling operation in the area had virtually ground to a halt, if he could only overcome the problem of landing cargoes successfully then moving the merchandise would be far easier than ever before due to the demand. Jacob would receive a far greater profit and have a monopoly over the whole market, controlling the prices of a wide range of smuggled goods and making a fortune in the process.

"The town had become a dangerous place with many people struggling for survival, stabbings and beatings became common practice after dark. Many houses were burgled but of course no one dared to go anywhere near Jacob Swift, even in desperate times people knew he was Bates' boy and anyone who dared to oppose him would face the wrath of the man with the dark eyes, a man who, however old, would always put the fear of life into even the most dangerous of men.

"Thomas pleaded with The Boy for permission to attack the customs men but without his consent no move was made.

Jacob wasn't keen on destroying property of the crown, as he was all too aware it carried a death sentence in British law and was equal to an attack on the King himself. Bates was equally stuck on how best to proceed. He'd never experienced such opposing forces and was unable to offer any words of advice.

"His back row continued to meet on a daily basis to discuss their limited options. Bribing was out of the question. Smollet had warned Jacob that the new officers were of a different generation, young, career-minded and eager to impress their superiors. Unfortunately, they were succeeding and as a result their confidence was growing daily. They couldn't be bought and even if they could it would be at a price way higher than The Boy could afford.

"Billy Bates had already met with several of his competitors who'd informed him that their operations were going under. They were good men who'd operated on this stretch of coast for donkeys' years only to have their livelihoods pulled from under their feet, leaving them penniless overnight. A handful of men had already been caught and faced deportation to the colonies on the other side of the Atlantic. Slowly everyone began to face the inevitable, times had changed and they'd have to try and seek an income elsewhere.

"Then, early one morning, Jacob took his father up to the wooden jetty at the head of the town so his old man could spend a few hours with his fishing buddies trying to hook that almighty catch. Like always Jim Robson, who seemed to grow bigger every time Jacob saw him, and Alfie Bicks, escorted him. The pair differed so much in appearance they looked comical. Jim with his youthful looks, short height, wide shoulders and barrelled chest. Alfie, the polar opposite, with his beard, height and skinny build. But they were as close as brothers and shared a common goal.

"Whilst The Boy stood talking to his father he watched the odd-looking pair larking around at the end of the jetty. Jim was hurling pebbles out into the sea and challenging Alfie to beat him on distance. Jacob watched as the stones hit the surface and disappeared under the murky depths, his mind wandered to all the cargoes that were being lost overboard into those same depths, costing him a future that he'd fallen in love with. Suddenly, out of nowhere, Jacob was hit with a thought that rapidly grew in his mind until he could no longer hold it in. 'My God,' he found himself mumbling.

"'You ok, son?' his father asked as he stared at his only child who had lapsed into silence once more looking lost in his own imagination as gulls squawked around him in the fresh, salty air. A moment later Jacob turned to his father with a sly grin etched on his face.

"'I'm good, Dad, I've just had an idea; will you be ok if I disappear for a few hours?' he asked.

"'No problem son,' his father replied as he began to adjust his fishing rod once more.

"Jacob spun around and shouted for his bodyguards who quickly stopped larking around and marched over to where he was stood.

"'We need to go visit Prosperity Farm immediately, I've just had an idea,' he informed them and within moments they'd climbed onto their horses and were galloping out of the town.

"In the middle of a field at the back of Prosperity Farm was a huge pond; it grew and shrank in size depending on the amount of rain that fell from the sky. At the moment the pond was large and, more importantly for what The Boy had in mind, it was deep. Around the pond stood four men, but two could have been considered boys if you'd judged them on age alone.

"Jacob, Jim and Alfie were joined by Havelock, the good-natured farmer who often helped the smugglers by loaning his cattle to help them bear the heavy weight of the goods they brought into the country.

"Jacob stood nearest the pond only a few feet from the bank. In his hands he held an 18-litre tub, which had been empty up until a moment ago when he'd filled it with water. Lying on the floor at his feet was a wooden crook around five feet in length which Jacob had requested off the farmer. He was just tying a piece of rope around the small barrel when his thoughts were interrupted.

"'I'm still confused about where this is leading, Swifty,' Alfie stated as he scratched his beard and stared at his young boss.

"'Just be patient and give me a moment,' Jacob replied before he hurled the wooden barrel out into the middle of the pond and watched as it crashed through the surface sending ripples circulating to the edges; a moment later the tub bobbed back up to the surface where it floated. Havelock, the farmer, was glancing at Alfie and Jim as if their young leader had lost his marbles; Jim and Alfie returned the expression equally confused until The Boy finally spoke.

"'Our problem,' Jacob began, pausing, 'well one of them at least is that when we do unload our goods overboard, which seems to be most of the time these days it floats on the surface like that,' he said pointing at the barrel bobbing up and down on the surface of the pond. 'It's far too easy for the Customs to locate and seize it,' he continued. The men were all nodding their agreement with The Boy's statement.

"'But if it isn't thrown overboard then our men get caught red-handed when that Customs cutter intercepts our vessel, which is a great deal worse,' Alfie pointed out.

"'Exactly,' Jacob said smiling.

"'You've lost me,' Jim added.

"'Me too,' the farmer chipped in.

"Jacob stood for a moment staring at each of the men stood around the pond before he began to speak once more. 'What if it didn't float on the surface but sunk disappearing completely under the sea?' he asked the trio of men whose expressions of confusion were slowly disappearing.

"'You want to sink it so the Customs can't retrieve it, then nobody wins,' Jim blurted out, happy that he'd finally clocked on to his boss' train of thought.

"Jacob smiled as he began to slowly tug on the rope in his hand reeling the small barrel towards him. 'Kind of,' he said. When the barrel was only a few feet from the bank Jacob leant down and picked up a rock which he fastened onto the rope using a fishing knot his father had taught him many years ago. Finally he flung the rock into the deep pond and it broke the surface with a splash, ripples spread everywhere and as the rock sank it pulled the barrel under with it, a moment later when the surface had calmed the tub was nowhere to be seen. Jacob turned to face the trio who stood looking astonished.

"'So you want to weigh the cargoes down so they can't be retrieved?' Jim asked, still a little unsure whether he understood what Jacob was thinking.

"'Kind of,' Jacob replied once again as he picked up the crook and poked it hook first underneath the surface of the pond. 'I want to anchor the cargo so if it does need to be thrown overboard we'll know exactly where it is.' He finished pulling the crook out of the water with the rope attached and hauling the tub out of the pond with a look of glee on his face.

"Alfie Bicks began to laugh and shake his head. 'It's got to be said you've amazed me this time lad, but what about the under currents in The Channel, it'll get dragged along the seabed over time and we won't be able to find it?' he asked.

"Jacob nodded slowly. 'That's true but if we drop them all tied together it'll weigh more and get dragged less. Plus we'll anchor them perfectly and drop it overboard in a specific location. Of course we'll need to retrieve them at the first opportunity. You have to admit it Alf it may just fool the Customs,' he said.

"'That it will,' Alfie agreed as he shook his head in amazement at The Boy's idea.

"It wasn't long after that the trio left Prosperity Farm thanking Havelock like always for his help, The Boy now had a thousand and one arrangements to make before that evening's landing and time was of the essence."

Chapter 16

"A short time later Jacob was pacing up and down in Billy Bates' study explaining his plan to Carp, Thomas, Jim, Alfie and Bates himself. Whilst The Boy strolled around the wooden table voicing his wild intentions for that evening's landing the rest of the men were deadly silent. At first they'd been laughing at the crazy idea but now they were deep in thought contemplating its chances of success.

"Finally the silence was broken by Bates himself. 'It's an unusual plan to say the least and, to be quite honest, I've never heard anything quite like it, but it just might work and if anyone could pull it off lad, you could,' he said as he watched Jacob stroll around the table through those dark eyes of his and lean in close towards him.

"'Bill, tonight's cargo is just brandy, 48 tubs worth. I'll tie them together in 4 sets of twelve and anchor them well,' Jacob said excitedly. 'Then as soon as I've unloaded them on the sandbank just off Deal castle that cutter will drop back I'm sure of it, they're as crooked as the rest, only interested in one thing and that isn't making arrests,' Jacob pointed out.

"'You're right there lad, they've had plenty of opportunities to intercept us out in The Channel but they hold back till we virtually hit the shore, all they've done so far is steal our merchandise,' Bill replied causing them all to voice their agreement with him.

"'Then me and a handful of my best men wait until the Customs Officers figure they've lost the load and sail away?' Carp asked the young leader who was nodding proudly 'Then we row out in a galley, hook the barrels up and stash em,' Carp finished. For a moment all the men were silent until Carp glanced over at Bates. 'I like it, Bill, it's daring,' he said before turning his attention back to The Boy 'But what about the riding officers on land?' he asked.

"Jacob smiled and looked over at Jim, Alfie and Thomas who were all grinning. 'Leave them to us, it's about time we returned the favour and made their lives a little harder,' Alfie said confidently, with that crazy look in his eyes. 'Don't worry they'll be miles off course and won't see a thing, that I can guarantee,' he concluded whilst Bates rubbed his chin deep in thought.

"'And Bill,' Jacob added. 'We can get £6 per tub instead of £4 when we sell it, that's an extra £96 on the load,' he reminded him. The room lapsed into silence at this whilst everyman present considered how needed that extra money was, the last few weeks had cost them all dearly.

"Finally Billy Bates spoke. 'The only risk that bothers me is you being aboard that cutter lad, I made a promise to your father that I'd look out for you and I don't break my promises for nobody, if you get caught, lad, then the games up for you,' he said rather honestly.

"Jacob absorbed the old man's words for a second. 'Bill, I appreciate your concern but you chose me because I know The Channel, I know exactly where and how to dump the cargo and above everything I know this will work,' Jacob said.

"Billy Bates smiled. 'You're growing into a man fast, lad, you go for it; I figure if it doesn't work then the game's up anyway so what have we got to lose,' he said looking around the table at the men who were once again nodding their agreement with serious expressions etched on their faces.

"Finally Jacob Swift began saying his goodbyes and shaking hands with the men he'd come to think of as brothers as if it was the last time he'd ever see them. A moment later he left the cliff-top house to begin his long journey. It was nearly midday already and he had to ride to the port of Sandwich to board Bates' clipper that would take him across The Channel to pick up the precious brandy.

*

"Hours later Carp and four of his best men were hiding in the dark between dozens of fishing boats that littered the beach near Deals Tudor castle, a stone monster built under the orders of Henry VIII in 1538 to protect the coastline from attack.

"A full moon shone its bright light down over the misty Channel and, from time to time, Carp aided by his pocket telescope managed to catch a glimpse of the smuggling vessel through the thick fog. Shielding out of the wind, his men sat on the shingle in silence under the shadows cast from the various boats that surrounded them.

"Finally Carp managed to catch a glimpse of the Customs cutter in the distance and hot on The Boy's tail. Carp watched anxiously as the two vessels played cat and mouse making their way to shore as he tried to block out the cold wind pummeling him from every angle, and sinking right through to his bones. Looking through his telescope he located where Jacob planned to unload the cargo overboard, it was only a few hundred metres in the ship's path and Carp estimated that the smugglers vessel would be over the drop zone in only a few minutes time.

"'Get prepared,' he warned his men as he prayed for Jacob's success.

"Only a few miles away, huddled around a small lamp at the head of the town, stood the half dozen riding officers; it had been an uneventful night for them so far. Conditions were terrible with visibility at a low. They were taking a rest from their usual patrol and, like always, were proudly wearing their military uniforms talking about their hopes for the future as their horses rested and drank water.

"Through the mist a lone figure appeared slowly walking towards them along the seafront, the officers wasted no time drawing their weapons. 'Who goes there?' the lieutenant ordered as he stepped forward and levelled his musket at the figure.

"'It's me, Smollet,' replied the familiar voice causing the lieutenant to re holster his weapon as the retired officer approached him.

"'I've heard news on the grapevine of a big cargo being

landed tonight,' Smollet warned the lieutenant whose ears pricked up at the unexpected news. Smollet felt a twinge of guilt from informing, his act of betrayal but loyalties were loyalties he reminded himself.

"'Who's running it?' the lieutenant demanded as he stared at Smollet with that look of contempt he only reserved for civilians.

"'Billy Bates and he's overseeing the landing himself,' Smollet replied knowing he'd just delivered the perfect bait. 'But they're landing in St Margaret's Bay, you'll need to move fast to catch them.'

"The Officer's eyes went wide at the mention of the notorious Billy Bates, Bill was their top target, something Smollet knew all too well, he also knew they'd receive a handsome bonus if they could catch him.

"'Thanks for the tip-off,' the Lieutenant said as he climbed onto his horse and shouted orders at his men. A moment later they galloped along the cobbles out of the town leaving Smollet alone in the fog. 'Just doing my duty,' Smollet muttered under his breath to no one in particular. He stood for a moment breathing in the fresh sea air before he heard footsteps behind him forcing him to spin around to face a sight that in years past would have sent shivers down his spine and put the fear of God into him.

"Appearing through the fog like the devil himself wearing a dark trench coat wrapped tightly around his huge frame stood Thomas, an orphan that had grown up on the streets robbing sailors at knifepoint to survive until he roused the attention of Billy Bates who saw his potential and took him under his wing, educating and housing him as he slowly cultivated his anger and turned him over the years into one of his most feared enforcers. The two men stared at each other for a moment before Thomas finally spoke. 'Good work, old man,' he complimented Smollet as he handed him some coins in his shovel-like hands. Pocketing the coins, Smollet quickly disappeared into the mist as Thomas began to jog along the sea front towards the wooden jetty sticking out into the rough Channel, reaching it he continued his run until he arrived at the very end where he pulled out a spout lantern from his pocket and lit it up.

"Thomas quickly flashed three sharp signals, but not out at the ocean like normal but directed towards the chalk cliffs south of the town. Extinguishing the lamp and placing it back into his pocket, Thomas slowly began to walk back along the wooden jetty, which creaked under his massive weight; he'd played his part in Jacob's plan even though he'd had his doubts. All he could do now was hope that The Boy's idea would work

*

Jacob Swift stood with the wind in his face on the deck of the small cutter surrounded by tubs that he'd finally finished tying together. He held on tight with his heart racing in his chest as the ship was battered at all angles by the rough sea. As a precaution he was wearing a cork life jacket just in case he accidentally got thrown overboard. The sea was a dangerous place and The Boy didn't want to add to the list of the lives it had claimed. In the back of his mind, Jacob knew that the next hour had the potential to go drastically wrong for him, costing him his freedom or even worse his life. He had taken a huge risk going through with the plan and hadn't banked on there being so much fog. He was struggling trying to locate the Custom's ship that had been trailing them at a distance for hours. Suddenly the fog parted for a second and he managed to catch sight of it causing him to gasp and sending a hit of adrenaline coursing through his veins.

"The ship was no longer at a distance but was beating down on their tails trying to intercept them before they reached the coast, spinning around and seeing the lights of the shore Jacob Swift pulled out his telescope and struggled to locate the landmarks he was planning on using to navigate the boat onto the drop off spot above the sandbank. Jacob shouted some orders to the ship's captain who quickly adjusted his course before he checked the barrels of brandy one last time.

"Glancing from the Custom's vessel, which was gaining

on them with every moment that passed, and the shore, The Boy prayed they'd make it to the sandbank in time. Otherwise his life as he knew it was about to take a serious turn for the worse. It was close way too close but Jacob took a deep breath and recollected Billy Bates' encouraging words, 'If anyone could pull it off lad, you could'.

*

"At the same time, several miles away, Alfie Bicks and Jim Robson were astride their horses high up on the chalk cliffs overlooking The Channel and the town. The odd pair looked like two sentinels, they were completely silent and on edge waiting for the signal so they could spring into action.

"'Come on, Tommy boy,' Alfie muttered under his breath before exhaling a lungful of air in anticipation. Several long moments later, the pair both saw three short flashes of light far away in the distance near the town's shore causing both men to break their silence with excitement.

"'They fell for it hook, line and sinker,' Jim said turning to his older accomplice who returned the smile.

"'It's time to lead them down the rabbit hole. You ready?' Alfie asked

"'Ready as ever,' Jim replied as they both fell silent listening to the rumble of horses' hooves over the cliffs from the half dozen riding officers, growing louder and louder as they got closer. Both men listened anxiously until Alfie decided they were close enough and dug his heels into his horse causing the animal to buck up on its hind legs and cry out in pain. A signal that would guarantee the riding officers' attention forcing them to give chase in the hope of catching the smugglers red-handed.

"Immediately Alfie and Jim began to gallop as fast as they could in the darkness across the cliff tops knowing that a handful of armed men were hot on their heels, but both Alfie and Jim took great satisfaction knowing that every step their horses took carried the riding officers further away from their friend Carp and his landing crew.

*

"Listening to his heart beating inside his chest as he scanned the horizon for landmarks, Jacob Swift knew the exact moment had arrived and he shouted the order to the ship's captain. Instantly The Boy was thrown about like a rag doll as the cutter made a dangerously sharp turn and began running parallel to the coast only a hundred or so metres off the shore. The ship's captain had carried out Jacob's crazy instructions with expert precision and as predicted the Custom's ship had dropped back not willing to follow the smugglers on a suicidal course.

"Jacob took deep breaths trying to settle his nerves as he watched the misty coastline that he knew so well passing by in front of his eyes, waiting for the clipper to align with Deal Castle's flagpole, which he was using as a navigation point.

"Jacob knew that, if he didn't do everything perfectly in the next thirty seconds, he would lose the entire load of brandy costing Bates a pretty penny.

"He'd convinced them all to go along with his crazy plan and he was grateful they'd listened and been willing to give him the benefit of the doubt. If it went wrong, the blame would fall at his feet and his alone. Jacob wasn't willing to let his friends down. Success was his only option. For Jacob Swift what happened next seemed to appear in slow motion and that's how he remembered it till the end of his days; it was a story he heard repeated so many times over the coming years that it became part of the legend of The Boy.

"As soon as the flagpole lined up and Jacob knew he was over the spot he'd agreed with Carp, he flung the first anchor over the side of the cutter closest to the shore, reaching for the next one his ears were filled with thunder as the anchor dragged its dozen strong load of barrels over the side of the small ship, each barrel bouncing on the ship's timber with a crash before it disappeared under the surface coming to a rest hidden on top of the sandbank only meters under Jacob's feet.

"Jacob himself had no time to waste as he frantically

unloaded all four of the anchors clearing the ships decks of forty-eight barrels of brandy in a matter of seconds. When the last barrel plopped under the surface silence returned and Jacob spun around smiling as he shouted orders at the ship's captain. Once again the small ship spun around taking a sharp turn back out into The Channel and as Jacob was flung about he managed to pull off the cork life jacket. Finally when the ship settled Jacob glanced at the captain who saluted him with respect before The Boy ran and leapt off the side of the ship into the fog and plunged into the dark murky water.

*

"Watching the spectacle unfold through his telescope, Carp stood observing it all in absolute amazement; it was one of the most bizarre sights he'd ever seen in his life. He'd watched as the Custom's ship had dropped back which was of no surprise. Carp knew the captain wouldn't dare take his vessel as close to the shore as the ship he was chasing. It was an act of suicide with the sandbanks and dozens of shipwrecks hidden under the surface. Unlike Bates' men the Customs didn't know the coastline, not like The Boy whose father had raised him to know the exact location of every wreck and bank that posed a risk.

"Carp watched as the tubs streamed over the cutter's side in a flash and, before Carp knew it, the smuggling vessel had swung back out into the channel. Now without lugging its cargo it was a good deal lighter and it quickly picked up speed once again grabbing the attention of the Customs' ship, which quickly attempted to resume its chase. Lowering his telescope Carp stood speechless for a moment as his men looked at him eager for instructions.

"Jacob had done it, fifteen years old and he'd outsmarted at least a dozen men. Carp had known Jacob for quite a while but it wasn't until that moment on the beach that he truly realized the potential that Bates had seen in The Boy.

"A second later, Carp kicked into action and ordered his men to carry the galley down to the waterline; minutes later they were rowing through the fog to where Jacob had unloaded and, before Carp knew it, he was pulling barrel after barrel of precious brandy up from the murky depths.

*

"It was Thomas who was the first to arrive at Billy Bates' headquarters. He found the old man seated in front of a blazing fire in complete silence. Thomas slid his huge frame into a chair and joined the man who'd virtually raised him, the man who was the closest thing he'd ever had to call family. Like Bates, Thomas's eyes were quickly drawn to the fire where the flames danced around. Thomas knew Bill better than anyone and he'd never seen the old rogue as on edge as he was that night. He informed Bill that his part in the plan had run smoothly and assured him not to worry. 'Jacob's a smart lad,' he'd said.

"Next to arrive and shattering the silence completely were Jim and Alfie; they thanked Thomas for a job well done before they recited their story about how they'd led the riding officers miles off course eventually losing them in Oxney woods. Billy Bates was beginning to perk up now with the realization that The Boy's daring plan may just have worked.

"Suddenly the group froze as footsteps were heard creeping up the stairs, Bates took a deep breath and braced himself for bad news but when the study's oak door swung open Carp strolled into the room with a beaming smile etched all over his face. It was a smile that said everything but Bates still had to ask,

"'How many did you retrieve?' he demanded as Carp continued to smile.

"'All forty-eight tubs, that's eight-hundred and sixty-four litres Bill,' he finally replied pausing whilst the men cheered in celebration. 'And it has to be said I watched Jacob unload with my very eyes; he left me speechless, that boy's something else.' At this Bates glanced over at Jim Robson, Jacob's best friend, before all the men shared that same look. Nothing more needed to be said about Jacob Swift. Every man present was

87

more than aware of what The Boy was capable of. He was both a thinker and a natural leader.

"A moment later one of Carp's men shuffled into the room lugging a barrel which brought on even more roars of celebration as it was cracked open and glasses were filled, but, before anyone drank a drop, they sat and waited for Jacob Swift, The Boy, their leader.

"It wasn't long until footsteps were heard once again on the stairs and Jacob strolled into the room, he'd been home and changed into his best suit and with his hair slicked back he looked much older than his years. The men drank late into the night and celebrated their victory over the Customs.

"In the early hours, Jacob was surprised to be taken aside by Thomas who rather honestly admitted that he'd had doubts about Jacob's leadership and that he'd secretly resented The Boy for his swift promotion in Bill's organization.

"'You see, Jacob, I always expected it to be me that took over from Bill when he retired,' the huge enforcer said in an emotional moment. 'But I now know why that couldn't be so and, from this day forth, I'm behind you all the way.' Jacob could see that it had taken a lot for Thomas to be so open and the pair made a secret pact that night that would last for many years to come.

"Jacob was praised and praised for his plan as the night wore on and the brandy found its mark. 'It was absolute genius,' a drunken Carp repeated on more than one occasion. But deep down The Boy knew it was only the beginning, the ball had begun to roll.

"Jacob had experienced a moment of clarity that evening whilst on the deck of that ship during all the chaos. He was aware that he was still too young but he knew that if he wanted to make something of himself in this world, then his moment had arrived sooner than expected. Jacob Swift planned on expanding Bill's Empire and taking over all smuggling operations in the entire area with immediate effect.'"

Chapter 17

"The Boy's plan was simple, daring and extremely dangerous. He knew that, to make it possible, it would take a lot of planning and the help and support of the whole crew, which thankfully was something he didn't doubt. Young Jacob had found a way of bringing goods into the country; it was far from straightforward but at the end of the day or night as the case may be it worked. He knew from Bill's contacts that most of the other operations on this stretch of coast were going under, so he figured that the opportunity to monopolize the market and control the prices of goods had presented itself. Jacob was fully aware that it would be impossible to exploit the opportunity if the details of his new landing technique got out; if that happened then, within days, every gang on the coast would follow suit and change their tactics, then he'd be back to square one. So, to keep his tactics secret, it was of the utmost importance that he only worked with men he could trust completely. But that was only the beginning; Jacob's plan had far more depth. When his mentor, Billy Bates, had informed him of his rivals approaches, with news that their operations were going under, The Boy's ears had pricked up.

"Jacob Swift was confident that if they were offered some sort of retirement package to keep them happy, then they'd be willing to offer their contacts and place their best men at The Boy's disposal. Most of Bates' rivals were as old as Bill himself; they didn't fancy taking the risks anymore, especially now that risk had grown far greater than ever before. Like Bill, most had earned their money over the years but they still felt responsible for the dozens of men who relied on them for an income.

"Jacob Swift knew he could solve everybody's problems by landing not one but ten cargoes a night. He could keep every man willing to risk their necks during the night hours happy with money in their pockets. At the present time, with nobody landing cargoes hundreds of men who smuggled for an income were suffering and day by day the situation was getting worse. Jacob knew he'd make a fair few enemies if he carried out his plan, he also knew that he had men who'd watch his back day and night, men like Alfie Bicks and Thomas.

*

"When Jacob woke up in the early afternoon after landing that first cargo of brandy, he lay in bed and within minutes he'd reached his decision.

"He crawled out of his bed, dressed and began a slow walk to Bill's headquarters perched high up on the chalk cliffs. Jacob still felt rough from the gutful of brandy he'd drunk the previous night but the long walk along the beach helped to clear his mind.

"The Boy, when he finally arrived at Bill's, was surprised to discover that the old man had been expecting him.

"That afternoon the pair sat and talked for hours. Jacob explained his plan in detail whilst Bill sat listening patiently and smiling throughout. Like Jacob, Bill knew that The Boy's time had come, and, as much as Jacob surprised Bill that day, Bates surprised The Boy. Billy Bates had worked hard all of his life and taken countless risks along the way, risks that had cost the lives of many of his friends.

"'It's time for me to take a backseat, I've no doubt you could land a dozen cargoes a night, I've no doubt you could do anything,' Billy Bates said in an emotional moment that brought tears to Jacob's eyes. 'From now on its gonna be you in charge,'

"'What!' Jacob found himself mumbling as he stared at the man who, along with his father, had taught him everything he knew in life.

"'The time's come, Swifty. If you lead them, my men will follow you all the way. Like me they believe in you, deep down you know that,' Bill concluded.

"So the pair sat sketching out a battle plan for The Boy's

future; Bates would always have some involvement one way or another but, from now on, it would be only as an adviser and the lion's share of profits would fall at Jacob Swift's feet. Billy Bates had spent a lifetime carving out a reputation in the town, a reputation that kept many people in line and the town was still as rough as ever. If the notorious Billy Bates announced his retirement and left The Boy's side completely then dozens of faces would emerge from the shadows. Billy Bates' reputation alone would keep them at bay but The Boy also planned on adding to the reputation he'd already began creating for himself.

"That afternoon, one of the first things the pair had planned was a meeting with everybody involved with the landing of the brandy the previous evening and explaining Jacob's intentions of swallowing up Bill's rivals. It was a meeting that most of the back row had expected and was great news to most who understood that expansion meant an increase in money as well as cargo. It was also great news for the likes of Alfie and Thomas who liked 'a bit of trouble' as they put it and trouble was the one thing everybody knew would be inevitable.

"Jacob explained his plan to the men he knew that it would be impossible to achieve without, for the next seven days no move would be made. They'd land their cargoes in the dead of night using only the most trusted of men and of course Jacob's new tactics. The Boy wanted to let everybody in the town suffer a bit more and, in the process, watch how desperate his rivals would become. Then, when he approached them with his offer, they'd snatch it up.

"So the days slowly passed by and, as Jacob's gang grew richer and stronger, everybody else grew poorer and weaker."

Chapter 18

"Every night for the following week Jacob and his men managed to land a cargo and, surprisingly, they found that the Customs' cutter didn't always even bother giving chase. However, the men took no risks, always sticking to their well-laid out plan they kept a close eye on the riding officers on land to make sure they were nowhere to be seen before signalling for their boats to venture close to the beach where they could unload the merchandise, just like they'd done countless times over the years.

"Now, though, the men were always ready to use Jacob's anchored technique and, out of the seven landings, they were forced to ditch the cargo overboard on only three occasions and every time they managed to retrieve the entire load without a glitch. It was having that ace up their sleeves, you see, that gave them peace of mind and as the days passed by their confidence grew and grew and they no longer feared the Customs' ship when it was spotted on the horizon.

"Jacob Swift had been studying the Customs every day and analysing the situation they faced; it became clear to him that when the Customs stopped getting the results or, more importantly, the merchandise they'd pull their men from the town and move to another stretch of coast where they'd make much more money on the side selling the black market goods they had confiscated. Back then smuggling wasn't just a menace to our stretch of coast, it had spread its tentacles all over the south-east of England.

"The Boy was both reassured that the Customs might not prove to be the problem he'd imagined and yet was still concerned. Because Jacob knew that if the Customs didn't prove to be a problem then he'd have to take much more ruthless action for his plan to work. When he had control of smuggling on the coast, he'd have to use the likes of Alfie and

Thomas to maintain his grip otherwise everybody would begin their own separate operations without passing some of their profits onto Jacob and he'd be back to square one.

"Over the previous days Billy Bates had been busy too, he'd been making sure that the cargoes they'd been landing went in the right direction and kept the right people happy. With the abrupt halt of smuggling, luxury items like tea and tobacco were virtually impossible to purchase in the town without paying the dreaded tax, the reason smuggling existed in the first place. Demand was extremely high and not everybody could be satisfied, not when The Boy was only pulling off one cargo per night but of course all that was about to change.

"Rumours were spreading through the town like wildfire. The streets were alive with them. It was no secret that someone was managing to beat the Customs and Excise at their own game and bringing goods across The Channel. Billy Bates, a man most people in the town feared, was working very hard to make sure that everyone knew that it was Jacob Swift or The Boy who was that someone. What's more, Bill was also spreading rumours that Jacob Swift was managing to achieve all of this because he had the Customs and Excise firmly in his pocket, he was a tough young man with brains to boot and feared nothing. The main reason these rumours were so successful was because they came directly from the mouth of Bates himself who everyone knew was a force to be reckoned with.

"Every day Jacob Swift was seen in the streets with men like Alfie Bicks whom everyone knew wasn't right in the head and Thomas, whose sheer size intimidated people, and that was before Billy Bates would even let him off his leash. People in the town were beginning to realize that it was Jacob Swift who now held that leash and, as a result, he was gaining power and respect daily.

"Bill was receiving messages from different crews who were struggling from the lack of work. They all wanted one thing, to sit down with The Boy. Everything was falling into place perfectly just how he'd foreseen it.

"Finally, Jacob decided it was time to make a move; the first crew he took over was known as the Bay Boys because they had a reputation for beaching their ships at high tide on the small stretch of sand at the mouth of the River Stour on the outskirts of Sandwich. Up until a few weeks ago when the dreaded Customs' ship turned up, they'd been led by a local man named Freddie Wilson. It had been Bates who'd encouraged Jacob to take on Fred's crew as apparently the pair went back a long way.

"'He's one of your own is Fred,' Bates had said in that rough old voice of his. 'Plus they've got two decent clippers that need to be put to use.' Apparently Fred had been in the game for nearly as long as Bill and he wanted out. When The Boy met Fred Wilson he understood immediately what Bill meant when he'd said that Fred was, 'one of your own'. He was a likeable man and Jacob got on with him instantly; the pair negotiated an arrangement that suited all parties, Fred would lease both his ships to Jacob who'd pay a generous amount to keep Fred happy in his long-awaited retirement.

"Fred had a dozen men whom he guaranteed were worth their weight in gold, Bates looked over the names with approval. They were good men who were both loyal to Fred and desperately in need of some income. Fred arranged a meet with his crew which The Boy attended, flanked by Thomas and Alfie, who both were carrying their bats concealed as usual. With the right words from Fred and Jacob the men were soon happy to go to work for The Boy they'd been hearing so much about lately.

"Jacob took no chances and had his men pull every one of Fred's crew aside to explain the consequences of betraying their new employer; not a single man doubted Thomas and Alfie's words but they knew times were harsh and above many things money bought loyalty. The Boy was one of the very few people with money to pay and at that meeting he bought a dozen men's loyalty.

"Jacob Swift wasted no time putting his two new boats to use and, for several weeks, he landed three cargoes a day; he mastered his plan and used one boat to distract the Customs and lead them away from the other two. Now, with far more cargo passing through his hands than ever before, The Boy found he had more money than he knew what to do with; he paid a handsome amount to Bill to honour the loan he'd received to buy his house overlooking The Channel. The rest he stashed up and watched as it grew and grew.

"Months passed by and Jacob's organization swelled and swelled as he swallowed up other crews with the promise of a steady income and, before long, The Boy had six vessels landing a wide range of goods virtually every day of the week.

"Around the town, Jacob Swift's reputation was growing and growing. He was considered a hero, The Boy who had saved many families from ruin. Now, when he strolled around the town's streets flanked by half a dozen of his best men, he was treated like royalty, people would come out of their houses to greet him and everybody wanted to be his friend.

"It took several years for Jacob to create the organization he'd dreamed of. Eventually he employed over two hundred of the town's toughest characters. Together Bill and Jacob planned operations, different locations to hide the endless flow of goods and outlets where they could shift them. Stories of The Boy who was leading an army drifted across the open fields of Kent, the garden of England, and into the heart of the city of London."

Chapter 19

Suddenly the mobile phone in Stan's rucksack began to spit out a tune which echoed through the still empty museum startling poor old Reg and making him jump. As he was pulled back to reality, he pushed his spectacles back up the bridge of his nose in an involuntary gesture. Whilst Stan rummaged frantically inside his bag to retrieve the phone, he muttered an apology. He felt bad for several reasons. Bizarrely he felt a twinge of guilt for having it switched on in the first place, it was like an unwritten rule in libraries, cinemas and museums you switched it off on entry. Stan knew that but his mum had told him she'd call and he daren't have switched it off. It wasn't just that though, as he fumbled through his rucksack for the phone he caught himself making a conscious effort to conceal the pieces of glass and the message he'd found on the beach and he felt really bad about that too.

Old Reg was pouring his heart out and Stan had never heard a story like it; he was enjoying it immensely. He didn't want it to stop and he didn't want Reg to think he was using or deceiving him. Stan would tell Reg all about the strange message in time when he'd heard the entire story, but he needed to hear all of it. His curiosity about what the message meant was growing and growing by the minute. Finally Stan's fingers reached the phone in his bag.

He watched as Reg took a well-earned sip of his tea which was now cold but still full. The old man had clearly forgotten it had been there. Come to think of it he'd been pretty caught up in his own narrative too; he seemed to enjoy the story as much as Stan and he knew it so well. He simply opened his mouth and it poured out.

'Unusual', Stan thought as he pushed it from his mind and put the phone to his ear. Immediately he heard his mum's voice. "About time, I was starting to worry," she said pausing as she laughed ever so slightly. Stan's mum never seemed to get angry, shout or punish him, not that Stan ever gave her reason to do so. It had been like that since his dad had left. Sometimes Stan was glad he'd just upped and left leaving them both alone because it had brought them closer together. Other times Stan missed him more than words could describe and prayed he'd come back. He loved his mum, she meant the world to him but she wasn't his dad.

"Sorry mum I've been kind of busy," Stan replied causing his mum to laugh.

"Yeah, what you been up to?" she enquired, pleased that he sounded much happier than he had over the previous week. Suddenly, though, Stan felt really awkward. Could he even tell his own mum the truth about the strange message in a bottle he'd found, certainly not now with Reg in earshot.

"I'm just looking around the old maritime museum," he answered

"Cool," his mum said after a moment, trying unsuccessfully to drag the word out and sounding just the opposite.

"Is that place still open? I can remember going there when I was a little girl with school. Anyway, my angel, could you pop back now we need to go check on Uncle Eddy," his mum informed him. Uncle Eddy was his mum's brother and a recovering alcoholic; he'd just been through a rough patch, and his mum wanted to keep a close eye on him. So Stan agreed and promised to be back within ten minutes before he hung up the phone and turned to Reg who was smiling in his direction. Stan felt frustrated to miss out on hearing the rest of the story today; he had to know what the message meant but, like Reg had promised, it was a long story and he would have to catch the rest at a later date. He had no choice.

Dread ran through Stan just like it had over the previous few weeks but now it had nothing to do with a certain bully named Daniel, he was now just an unpleasant memory in Stan's mind. The thought of never knowing what happened to The Boy and what the Eye of the Serpent actually meant scared Stan. What if the old man didn't ever finish the story and Stan spent his life wondering 'what if'? Plucking up courage, Stan turned to Reg and asked if it would be ok if he returned the following morning; he hoped with all his heart that the old man would be ok with it.

Reg couldn't help but laugh at the serious expression on the young man's face, he was so determined to learn about Swifty, the local hero that time had forgotten. Reg couldn't help but wonder why? But he told Stan that it would be a pleasure, Reg had enjoyed the morning too. He'd found that, as he'd gotten older and older as the years ticked by around him, Reg found himself feeling even more useless and redundant. He'd spent a lifetime chasing a dream and looking for that light at the end of the tunnel only to eventually question whether it had even existed in the first place; sometimes he couldn't help but think his life had just been one big waste of time.

*

That evening Stan lay in his bed fantasizing about what it would have been like to live in Jacob Swift's day. Life was much different back then with danger at every corner.

He puzzled once again about what the strange message could have meant up to the point where he began to drive himself a little crazy. The Eye of the Serpent! What did it mean? In the end he reassured himself that, come the morning, he'd hear the rest of the story and if he was really lucky he might find out.

That thought made him feel a great deal better and eventually he drifted off into a deep sleep with a smile on his face dreaming of adventures out at sea and of course... Treasure. Daniel Ryan hadn't even crossed his mind.

*

The next morning when Reg unbolted the museum's main door at 10 am, for once somebody was already waiting eagerly. Secretly this made old Reg happy. The story he was in the middle of telling young Stan had consumed Reg's entire life in his younger years. When Reg was a young boy and his mother had told him the story of Jacob Swift and the Eye of the Serpent for the first time, just like her mother had many years before, it amazed him and he'd been unable to think of anything else. He began his own research within weeks trying to discover any clue as to whether it existed in the first place and where The Boy could have stashed it, but it was like the treasure had just vanished and this only backed up the theory that the notorious smuggler had been used as a scapegoat. In the end Reg had to come to the frustrating conclusion that, if it had existed, only Jacob knew its whereabouts and he'd taken it to a watery grave. For Reg, it was reassuring to see someone else fascinated by the story. It made him feel not so alone in the world. However Reg was puzzled about where Stan had heard the name 'Swifty' in the first place, he decided that the young man must have read about it in a local history book. Stan was a curious lad but Reg decided there was definitely no way Stan knew about the treasure. Reg wondered whether to include it in the story at all and decided to, he liked Stan. Jacob Swift had been mentioned in dozens of books by local authors over the years and never very accurately, much to Reg's anger. There had been no mention of treasure. Powerful people had covered their tracks back in the day to avoid a scandal and they'd done a good job of it too.

Stan strolled into the museum with a big grin and took a seat. He began to rummage in his bag for what seemed like an eternity.

"I have a surprise for you, Reg," he said before finally pulling out a thermos flask.

"I made some coffee for us," he said making Reg smile.

"So where was we... Jacob had taken over lots of other operations and had become the main man in the town." Reg chuckled and took a seat next to Stan who smiled as he handed him the flask.

Chapter 20

"Several years had passed by and Jacob Swift was now only The Boy in name. He'd grown into a dashing young man with shoulder-length blond hair and blue eyes. He was always impeccably dressed, well-mannered and, with the wealth he'd accumulated too, he was the most desirable bachelor in town. Women would constantly seek his attention, the rich too. Daughters of wealthy merchants and landowners who'd heard the rumours about Swifty, the King of Smugglers, as some people called him. Of course these young rich women only wanted a bit of rough; they never saw a future with The Boy, they just wanted a story to tell over dinner with their rich friends. Jacob knew this, he wasn't easily fooled but, like everything else Jacob used it to his advantage making contacts among the rich and powerful who trod paths far removed from his own. He never seemed to get too close to women though, some say it was because he had grown up with his dad alone and surrounded by fishermen he didn't know how to deal with women emotionally. Others say that The Boy feared women because of his mother's death during his birth which was a weight he carried around with him his whole life. Personally, with what I've learned over the years, I go with the latter, but what is evident is that Jacob Swift did know how to seduce women to gain information if nothing else.

"Jacob wasn't the only person to turn into a man, his pal Jim Robson had too but, unlike Jacob, Jim had turned into a mountain, he was cube-shaped with shoulders that swelled with pure muscle. Jacob and the rest of the back row would often joke that Jim and Thomas were twins that had been separated at birth. Few though would ever tease either man face-to-face; like Thomas, Jim had been growing quite a reputation in the town.

"A few years previously when Jacob had first taken over

and expanded Bates' empire or The Boy's as the case had been. It had been a struggle to maintain it but Jacob had sunk his teeth in and refused to let go, as a result all of his enforcers including Jim had been kept very busy. Over the years countless men tried to muscle in on The Boy's territory. Jacob always explained that they were welcome to smuggle on the coast but if they did they did so for him. He never asked but always told and, after explaining the consequences, most men usually fell into line. It was always just business for The Boy and nothing personal, you were either with him or against him and that was something no one fancied.

"It was well-known in the area that Jacob had around three hundred men working for him and every one of these would stick a blade in you without a second thought at The Boy's say so. But the biggest reason Jacob Swift was so successful was because he understood money and how much people depended on it to survive; he quickly realized that it was an easy way of controlling people. 'Whoever pays the piper picks the tune' and when that didn't work he could fall back on the likes of Jim, Thomas and Alfie Bicks who were always happy to swing their bats in his name.

"So you could say that times were good for The Boy. He'd paid off his loan to Billy Bates who was still around and enjoying his retirement. Bill was an educated man not that anyone in the town ever realized. Bill had cultivated an image for himself in the area and few people ever got to know the real Bill. The old man with eyes like marbles would spend most of his days seated up on the cliffs near his house watching the movement in The Channel through his telescope or reading a book. Jacob would often seek his guidance and, once a week without fail, the pair would dine in one of the towns fancy restaurants alongside equally wealthy people with whom they had very little in common. Bill was working-class to the roots and knew he didn't belong in such fine establishments but who in their right mind would have ever told him that. Jacob liked to be seen out and about among the right people, after all Bill had taught him the power of reputation and The Boy figured he had no problem controlling the working classes. Money was a powerful weapon, it was the rich he figured he needed to keep an eye on.

"The years hadn't been too good to Bill; he'd worked a hard life and his back often ached but he still managed to put the fear of death into people. Most of his generation were still kicking about and they remembered some of the things he'd done in the town both good and really bad. Whilst the pair ate their meals or strolled through the town's cobbled and dangerous streets, people would approach them constantly to wish them well.

"One day as they sat and ate Bill turned to Jacob. 'There is a thin line between fear and respect, lad, make sure you always know which is which,' he said and Jacob understood what he meant immediately. It made The Boy feel sad for the man that had taught him his trade. Jacob Swift had been busy using some of his wealth to buy power which was something Bill had never done and didn't agree with. Times were changing real fast and, even though Jacob respected Bates more than most men, he understood that Bill was old school. Jacob knew that, as times changed, he needed to change with them. If he stuck to his principles and never altered his methods his empire would be washed away with the next tide. Jacob paid local politicians and the town's magistrate, even the mayor was in his pocket and would often praise 'Our young friend' during his speeches knowing that everyone in the town knew exactly to whom he was referring. It was mutually beneficial for the mayor. With Swifty's support it guaranteed the support of all of his people. The mayor knew that amounted to most of the town, anyway, so he figured he couldn't lose. Nothing ever happened in the town without Jacob's knowledge or permission as was often the case and he always used, knowledge to his advantage.

"One day, one of his many contacts on the streets fed him some information about one of the town's vicars who had been visiting the working girls of Portobello Court most evenings. This made The Boy chuckle, 'it takes all sorts' he thought. The next day he sought confession from that vicar and in confidence informed the man of the cloth of what he'd learnt.

From that day on he was using the church's crypts to hide brandy, wine and tobacco on holy ground where no one would ever look. Storing it underground where the temperature was constantly low also had the extra advantage of keeping the goods fresh. That same vicar also began to praise 'Our young friend' during his sermons too which was great for Jacob Swift as it gained even more support from the local community.

"One day Havelock, the farmer who Jacob had formed a great relationship with and been especially generous to bought The Boy a pure white horse at an auction. It was thoroughbred and caught everyone's attention as Jacob would trot through his streets on her with half a dozen of his bodyguards, tough men who rarely left his side.

"Everything was going well for Jacob, his dream that he'd harboured since he was a kid, when he'd worked in The Channel with his father fishing, had come true. Then one summer afternoon when Jacob visited Bates' headquarters with Alfie and Thomas they found the body and from that point things took a turn for the worse."

Chapter 21

"Alfie Bicks had been the first to stroll into the study at Bill's headquarters; he was closely followed by Jacob and Thomas. The trio had been in hot debate about something or other but their conversation had come to an end rather abruptly. The notorious smuggler Billy Bates, whose name caused the hairs to prick up on the backs of most men, was lying on his back. His mouth was slightly open as were his eyes with those black marbles of his staring up at the ceiling. In one of his hands he clutched a book on poetry.

"For a moment that lasted a lifetime, all three men stood speechless and rooted to the floor like statues, then Thomas who stood nearest the door barged past Alfie and Jacob and dropped to his knees, he shook Bill's lifeless body before letting out a wail of grief as tears rolled down his face.

"Jacob Swift stood watching the scene in front of him unravel as if it was a dream. Thomas was a man known to be an animal with a heart of stone and Jacob was shocked to see him crying like a baby as he gripped one of Bill's hands. The Boy had never seen his fearless bodyguard look even slightly vulnerable and, up to that moment, he'd doubted it had even been possible.

"Alfie prodded Jacob's shoulder pulling him from the trance-like state he'd found himself in. The Boy quickly moved to Thomas' side and, a moment later, the huge man had wrapped his bear-like arms around him and was crying with his head on Jacob's chest. Alfie stood staring at Bill's body, his eyes showed little emotion. Jacob had no doubt that Alfie had loved Bill dearly. He'd worked for him for over fifteen years. But Alfie's heart had grown cold many years ago if it had even existed in the first place.

"For Thomas, the great Billy Bates had been much more than just a boss, when the ruthless enforcer had been an 11-

year-old boy and living rough on the town's streets he'd taken many risks to survive. Thomas had been raised as an orphan but, as soon as he was old enough, he'd escaped from the institution he'd been forced to call home, a place where abuse was a fact of life. One day Thomas made the mistake of robbing one of Bill's men at knifepoint. The story flew around the town like wildfire and everyone held their breath expecting Billy Bates' vicious response. When Bill finally tracked Thomas down and found him living under a wooden jetty wearing only rags he did something no one expected and offered the boy a home and security which were things that most people took for granted. Thomas had been dealt some harsh blows in life and had been mistreated by the very people who were supposed to be caring for him. Billy Bates had been like a father to Thomas.

"Eventually Alfie summoned a doctor who pronounced Bill as dead, the cause was likely to be heart failure and the doctor reassured the men that Bill hadn't suffered. It had come on suddenly hence the book which was still clutched in his hand.

"For Jacob Swift, Bates' death had a different effect than either of his bodyguards. Death scared Jacob, it had taken his mother from him and he had no idea how to deal with it. Initially, when they'd found the body, Jacob had been in shock and had focused his attention on supporting Thomas who had clearly needed it. But, as the days passed before the funeral, Jacob felt emotions he'd never felt before; he felt like a part of him had been taken away and he was having serious doubts whether he could carry on leading his men. He bottled all this up. He knew he needed to remain strong in public as all eyes were on him both inside and outside of his organization. Up until then, The Boy had never realised how much he'd relied on Bill as the years had passed. He'd rarely needed the old man's help but just knowing that he'd been there to offer advice in his croaky old voice had been all the peace of mind that Jacob Swift had ever needed. Now all that was gone, he had three-hundred men at his side but he felt so alone.

"When the body had been found, one of the first things

that Jacob Swift had done was arrange an emergency meeting with his back row. He felt it was important that they were the first to know. Like most things even the back row had expanded over the years. There were several new faces that had hardly known Bates personally but, of course they'd heard his name, very few in the town hadn't. All the old faces were still kicking about and, as you'd imagine, they were devastated by the news. Billy Bates had been much more than just a smuggler. He'd been a trusted friend, someone whose promise counted for something. He was a man of honour who had done as much good as he had bad.

"It didn't take long for news of his death to get around the town, whispers travelled from ear-to-ear and tavern-to-tavern through Deal's cobbled streets. Everyone wanted to pay their respects and offer their condolences. Many Jacob doubted had even known the great man and were simply trying to score points in The Boy's eyes, but death was like that, it brought people out of the woodwork and that, more than anything, was what Jacob Swift was about to learn.

"Bill's funeral service was a huge affair. It was the biggest the town had ever seen with hundreds of Bill's friends travelling from all over the county to pay their last respects. It was held in St George's Church with people filling up the graveyard and even the adjoining streets, many The Boy didn't recognize but there were dozens of people that he did, people Bates had introduced him to over the years.

"During the service, Jacob stood at the front of the church next to his father who shed a tear for his old childhood friend; they were surrounded by the back row, Havelock, the farmer who had always been a close friend of Bill's and a dozen tough-looking bodyguards. The Boy knew people would be looking his way for any sign of weakness and it was important for him to show his strength not only to outsiders but to anyone else in his own organisation that had their doubts.

"The actual service was short. Billy Bates had never been a holy man and everybody knew it. Several people stood up and reminisced about happy times they'd shared with the old weathered-looking man who was lying in the casket at the front of the church with his eyes closed, resting peacefully at last. After the service, the coffin was carried through the streets Bill had spent his life in. Anchored to the wooden jetty at the head of the town were several of The Boy's vessels.

"The coffin was loaded aboard alongside two dozen of Bill's closest friends and they sailed out into the English Channel. When Billy Bates' coffin was put into the water, it sunk under the surface and every man on board shed a tear for the man they'd loved, happy though that the great man's body was resting where it belonged. Bill had loved the ocean and often joked that he had salt water for blood.

"In the build-up to the funeral, Jacob had spent a lot of time alone with Thomas, both men had suffered a great loss and leaned on each other for support. In those few days the pair formed a bond so great it would last for the rest of their lives. It was destiny because both men were about to stand together and fight a war with a small army that had gathered in the shadows."

Chapter 22

"It was two days after the funeral when it all began and the threat first emerged. Jacob Swift hadn't lost a cargo in a long time and when he had it was always due to poor weather conditions and the merchandise had become ruined. That day though he lost an entire cargo and one of his teams were robbed at gunpoint. It was summer at the time and the sun wasn't setting until gone nine so the landings weren't even beginning until around eleven.

"That night The Boy had arranged for five separate cargoes to land on our shores, all from different vessels at different times on separate sections of coastline beginning at Sandwich Bay and stretching all the way to the chalk cliffs at Kingsdown. All-in-all though it hadn't been that busy a night for Jacob whose many teams often landed a dozen loads in one evening, but Jacob figured that the thieves hadn't the patience to wait for the ideal load. With Bill's death they wanted to strike while the iron was hot and catch The Boy whilst he was most vulnerable.

"It was rumoured that Jacob's empire had been dealt a harsh blow with the loss of the notorious Billy Bates; it had been weakened and the moment for his enemies to crawl from the shadows and attack had arrived. Whilst Jacob's operations had gone from strength to strength over the years, his empire had swelled, but so had his profits. The Boy always paid his men well but it was no secret around the town that Jacob Swift, the fisherman's son, was making a fortune for himself. Money and greed seemed to go hand-in-hand, but so did greed and risk. The time had arrived for a small gang to take that risk and do what others feared, take on 'The Boy'.

"The raid had been well-planned, that much was clear from the beginning. One of Jacob's crews had picked up a cargo of tobacco and red wine; it wasn't a huge load and had only required six men to transport the merchandise, backed up by four with bats. The team had loaded up the goods on the beach and began to make their way across the marshland past the ruins of Sandown Castle when the thieves had struck. They'd been lying in wait in the long grass and, as soon as Jacob's team had wandered into a good enough position, the thieves had sprung up and overpowered them with little effort. Thankfully, Jacob's men who were armed only with bats realised they didn't stand a chance against firepower and didn't put up too much of a fight. This came as a relief to Jacob; he figured he could afford to lose a load but good men were priceless.

"The thieves had wasted no time relieving Jacob's men of their merchandise before tying them up. They were two dozen strong and well organized. It wasn't just a random hit by opportunists. It had clearly been very well-planned. The thieves wore black balaclavas covering their faces. They had brought rope and enough men to haul the goods out of the marsh but what shocked everyone the most was the stark message that one of the bandits had delivered before making it off on foot into the darkness. 'Tell Jacob Swift there's a storm brewing,' he'd warned.

"Hours later, as Jacob heard the entire story, whilst seated at the huge table in Bill's study surrounded by his back row he didn't quite know what to make of it. Personally for Jacob it couldn't have come at a worse time, he was battling with his own crisis of confidence but he knew how to control his emotions and he never gave away even the slightest hint of the troubles he was dealing with deep inside.

"Out of the corner of his eye he could see Thomas's huge frame jammed into a chair, he was gritting his teeth and clenching his fists so hard they'd turned white. The Boy knew he wasn't the only one dealing with their demons. In front of the table stood Eric Decan, he was a good lander who'd worked in the smuggling game for the best part of twenty years, the last two for Jacob.

"'How many did you say there was?' Alfie Bicks asked looking outraged that someone had the audacity to attempt such a stunt.

"'At least twenty, maybe more,' Eric said. 'But only six or so were armed.'

"Jacob could see that Eric was a little shook up. 'Still half a dozen guns is more than enough.' The Boy stated to make him feel better, he figured that, likewise, Eric had been through more than enough for one evening.

"'And you didn't recognize any of them?' Jim Robson asked.

"Eric Decan looked straight into Jacob's eyes. 'It was dark and they were covering their faces,' he pleaded.

"Jacob nodded and racked his brain. 'What about their voices did you recognize any?' he finally asked, Eric put his head down shamefully. 'I can't say I did,' he said.

"The room fell silent for a moment until Jacob Swift turned to his men 'Any thoughts?' he asked. Once again the room fell silent for several long moments before they broke into a discussion that lasted late into the night. Alfie Bicks began by pointing out that whoever was responsible was fairly local, they knew too much and the timing was so close to Bates' death it stunk to high heaven.

"'You think they have someone on the inside?' Carp asked aloud to nobody in particular but echoing every man's thoughts.

"It was Jacob who eventually answered. 'It's likely, I think it's best to assume they have,' he said before turning his attention to Alfie who appeared deep in thought.

"'I want every man on that run questioned, somebody must know something,' Jacob ordered, Alfie nodded slowly as he twisted the end of his ginger beard with that crazy look of his etched on his face.

"'No problem,' he finally replied.

"'So we have a gang who have been waiting for their moment to cause some trouble, that much we do know,' Jim Robson pointed out, the room fell silent as every man contemplated Jim's words.

"'They can't be from the town we have people everywhere,' Alfie said before Carp turned to Jacob and looked The Boy in the eye. 'Whoever did this, Swifty, it's just the beginning you know that don't you?' he asked and Jacob nodded, he knew only too well.

"'We have to get prepared,' Carp continued.

"'And armed,' Alfie chipped in, the lanky bodyguard who'd watched Jacob's back since day one had warned The Boy on several occasions about the need to carry firearms. Guns were becoming the norm as times changed. Knives and bats were no longer a strong enough deterrent. Jacob had dozens of contacts and could easily obtain the best muskets and rifles on the market but he'd been hesitant. With a gun in your hand it was much too easy to kill a man, it took a lot of discipline to carry one. With a bat it was different you could get your message across without causing mortal harm which was something The Boy knew was always bad for business. Now, though, Jacob Swift had no qualms about investing in firepower, he was going to arm his men to the teeth.

"Finally, The Boy spoke with all the confidence and leadership that Billy Bates had seen in him that first night when they'd met on the beach. 'I want a team of men assembled, trusted men, at least forty of our best. If they're going to come after our loads we're going to wait and be ready,' Jacob stated to the room who were all nodding their heads in agreement, all apart from Thomas who seemed lost in a world of his own. 'I want every man in this room to put their ears to the ground, if this gang are from this area then somebody in this town knows about them. Two dozen men can't move around unseen. I want to know where they're hiding out and who's helping them whether they're feeding them with provisions or information. Do whatever you think is necessary and we'll meet early tomorrow afternoon to make preparations for that night's landings.' Jacob finished breaking up the meeting.

"Everyone slowly rose to their feet. It had been a long night. When everyone had shuffled out of the study, only Thomas remained. Eventually he looked up at Jacob through eyes that were clouded with the hatred and anger brewing up inside him.

"'When we find out who they are I need some time alone with them,' was all the squat enforcer said through clenched teeth. They were words that chilled Jacob to the bone, but he nodded his agreement knowing that, for Thomas, aggression was the only way he could deal with his grief."

Chapter 23

"When Jacob finally climbed into bed that night, he tossed and turned pondering his many problems and how best to deal with them; eventually sleep found him, but as soon as the new day broke he was wide awake and determined to take action. The Boy still hadn't really dealt with Billy Bates' death. The old man had been a mentor, friend and a father figure. The troubles Jacob was facing just gave him the excuse he needed to avoid it. Jacob knew he had to keep himself busy to take his mind off dealing with the grief that was consuming his heart.

"At around eight a.m. Thomas and Jim Robson arrived at his town house and, from their appearance, Jacob knew immediately that like him they hadn't slept easily. The trio, along with Jacob's father, sat and drank tea as they looked through the huge bay windows out at The Channel and the many different ships navigating her, they discussed their general plan for the morning before the trio mounted their horses and trotted slowly through the town's streets.

"Many people were up and about already preparing their businesses for the day's trading, washing their front steps or walking and brushing the night's sleep away. Whatever their purpose, it pleased The Boy who knew that tongues would certainly be wagging in the wake of the great Billy Bates' demise. Jacob wanted to send a clear message to everybody that whatever was happening he was far from scared and was in the town to stay. He'd been very lucky to be taken under the wing by a man as powerful and wise as Bill, but he had worked hard for what he had and he wasn't willing to let it go for anybody. So that morning, when he rode through the streets that he'd come to think of as his own on his pure white horse, heads turned, but Jacob made sure that he kept his held high.

"The first meeting Jacob had that morning was with the town's magistrate. An overweight, lazy man named Theodore

Rawlings who was rotten to the core. Generally the magistrate did more bad than good in the town and Jacob trusted him about as far as he could spit, but the man could obtain information that others couldn't. Information that often proved valuable to Jacob who liked to keep one step ahead of the game. The corrupt magistrate was only interested in one thing… money, and worked for whoever paid him. The Boy figured that it would be best if that person was him.

"The magistrate met Jacob and his two bodyguards up near the wooden jetty at the head of the town. Jacob always met him in public. He didn't trust Rawlings but he also figured that it could only benefit him if people knew he had the magistrate in his pocket, and one thing that Jacob Swift had learnt about the town was that people talked. Jacob began by explaining about the previous night's events whilst Theodore Rawlings stared at The Boy as if he couldn't have cared less. When Jacob finally asked if he had any information, the fat magistrate casually shook his head which angered Jacob who was beginning to realise that he'd been wasting his money buying off the law in the first place and that maybe Bills attitude towards bribing people had been the right one.

"'I haven't heard anything but I'll look into it,' Rawlings said, pausing with a bemused look on his face. 'You know thefts happen in this town all the time' Jacob spun around to face the corrupt man who still had an expression on his face that The Boy couldn't quite place.

"'Not to me they don't!' Jacob spat out before he climbed up onto his horse and nodded to his bodyguards that it was time to leave. 'I want information, you know how to contact me,' he said before riding off with Thomas and Jim in tow hoping that Alfie Bicks was having more luck questioning the men who'd worked on the previous night's landing. It was only when Jacob Swift was a distance away that the magistrate laughed to himself. 'Oh I'll be contacting you boy, don't you worry,' he muttered under his breath.

*

"Alfie Bicks paced up and down, occasionally glancing over at the man seated on the chair in the corner of the room whilst he twisted his beard. The man looked scared but he had no need to be, like all the other men who had worked on the dreaded load the previous evening, he knew nothing. That was clear enough.

"Alfie pulled at his beard puzzled as he tried to figure out how he was going to discover the identity of the traitor inside Jacob's organization. It could have been any of the three-hundred or so men in the town that relied upon The Boy for a living. It was like finding a needle in a haystack. Whatever happened, though, if they found the bandits or not, they needed to discover the Judas among their own men and Alfie Bicks wouldn't rest until they had.

"The tall bodyguard knew that if he had five minutes alone with anyone of the bandits he'd learn everything he needed to know, but would he ever get that opportunity? Alfie certainly hoped so. Then a face popped into Alfie's mind. A man's face with a savage scar running all the way down to his chin, Alfie recollected the night many years ago when Bill had given him that scar. Then suddenly an idea struck Alfie Bicks, someone knew something and that someone was an enemy rather than a friend. Alfie couldn't think of a greater enemy. The man with the scar down his face was always in The King's Head on the outskirts of the town; he hadn't dared venture further since Bill had warned him all those years ago.

*

"Meanwhile Jacob, Thomas and Jim Robson had made their way over to Sandwich to pay a visit to a wealthy and powerful merchant named Robert Planter. He had been a lifelong friend and ally of Bill's. Jacob knew the man well and had spoken to him only a few days previously at Bill's funeral. Bob Planter was a wealthy man and mixed in many social circles. He owned an import/export operation from the docks on the banks of the River Stour in Sandwich trading mainly in slate from Wales, coal from Northumberland and timber from the Baltic. He was well-dressed and well-spoken and, on the surface, it would have been hard to figure that he even knew men like Billy Bates. Generally Planter ran his business legitimately but sometimes he dabbled in the grey areas as Bates had put it.

"When The Boy arrived at Planter's office, the merchant rose to his feet and greeted Jacob so warmly that The Boy knew in his heart that the journey hadn't been wasted. The pair talked briefly about the funeral service and the great man that had brought them both together. Eventually, Jacob got round to the purpose of his visit.

"'Bob, I'm experiencing a few problems at the moment,' he admitted

"Robert Planter looked deep in thought for a split second before he looked Jacob in the eyes. 'How can I help?' the merchant asked concerned.

"'I need some firepower,' Jacob stated.

"Robert Planter stared at the young man in front of him with a sad look etched on his face. 'Bill was like a brother to me and you were like sons to him,' he replied as he slowly looked at Thomas and then Jacob in turn. 'Of course I can help.'

*

"When Alfie Bicks strolled into The King's Head tavern on the outskirts of the town he realized he'd made a great mistake before the door had even swung shut behind him, Alfie had unknowingly walked directly into the lion's den and he cursed himself for not bringing some back up. The tavern was packed to the hilt with men who wouldn't hesitate sticking a knife in his back.

"The man he'd been looking for, Henry Cutler, saw Alfie from across the bar and his mouth fell wide open in astonishment. Cutler had worked for Billy Bates for a brief period and had managed to cause a great deal of trouble for the old man with the eyes like marbles. In the end Bill had taught him a lesson, setting an example in the process to anyone else in the town who dared to challenge him, but that was more than ten years in the past.

"Now though, as Alfie stared around the tavern's packed interior it wasn't Cutler's face that Alfie saw it was several dozen dangerous men's, men who were from out of town. They all shared that same look with virtually identical features and Alfie Bicks knew immediately who they were; over the years he'd fought with many of them. They were the Jenkins family and suddenly the pennies began to drop. Alfie could only stand with his mouth open as every man in the tavern fell silent and flashed evil looks his way. The Jenkins crew's main base was further up the coast but they had members of their clan scattered everywhere. In the years past they were a force to be reckoned with but then the law had caught the man who'd led them, he'd been locked up in the clink before eventually being put on a slave ship and banished to the colonies to face a lifetime of hard labour for his savage crimes. Soon after that, the Jenkins family lost their grip on the area, finally ending their reign of terror.

"It was Henry Cutler himself who finally broke the silence as he stood to his feet.

"'Well, well if it isn't Alfred Bicks you really must be as crazy as they say to stroll in here as bold as brass,' he stated as every man rose to their feet looking in his direction. Alfie could only stare Cutler in the eyes keeping his mouth shut as he felt around for the handle of the razor in his pocket.

"Suddenly the crowds parted as a huge figure began to make its way across the tavern towards Alfie stopping only when their faces were inches apart and causing Alfie Bicks' heart to miss a beat. With Alfie's huge height it was rarely that he looked people in the eye but with the man in front of him he had no trouble.

"Big Ronnie Jenkins stood at six foot seven like Alfie, but unlike Alfie the leader of the Jenkins family was far from skinny. He was built like a packhorse and much bigger than Alfie could remember. The years of hard labour at least had some rewards.

"Alfie Bicks feared no man but if he had it would have

been the man in front of him.

"'It's been a long time,' Ronnie said with a sinister smile on his face, the huge man had a wide jaw and a nose that had been broken more than once.

"'I thought they banished you to the colonies?' Alfie asked trying to buy some time as he desperately tried to find the handle of the razor in his pocket.

"Ronnie Jenkins laughed to himself for a moment causing many of his clan to snigger. He looked around the tavern at his brothers, cousins and nephews. A moment later he stared at Alfie and the smile had vanished completely.

"'Is that why you thought you could slap Bobby around, eh?' he asked through gritted teeth. Alfie looked around the tavern finding Bobby Jenkins face among the crowd. That night on the beach when Jacob had first started out in his smuggling career and Bobby had turned up drunk came flooding back to the tall bodyguard. Alfie understood, the Jenkins motto was power in numbers and he had to admit that they certainly had that, Alfie's fingers finally came to grip on the handle of his cutthroat razor. He looked back into Ronnie Jenkins' eyes. Alfie knew that, if he took out Big Ronnie he wouldn't leave the tavern alive, but it was a price he was willing to pay for Jacob Swift.

"Big Ronnie wasn't stupid though. He'd known Alfie back in the day and was well aware of his reputation for knives. The leader of the Jenkins family took a big step backwards out of reach and before Alfie was able to react, the first bat hit him on the back of the head sending him sprawling to his knees. A moment later half a dozen of the Jenkins family were raining down blows with fists and boots, including a drunken Bobby who had been waiting a long time for his revenge.

*

"Jacob stood at the head of the table in the study at Bates' headquarters surrounded by his back row. The table in front of him was covered in various rifles, muskets, the cases the guns came in and of course the straw that had been used as a

118

packing material.

"The merchant, Robert Planter, had been true to his word providing forty weapons to Jacob at the price he'd bought them for. Jacob had tried to force Planter to take more money but the merchant had outright refused in honour of his late friend Bill. The men were busy practising loading and cleaning the guns as they talked about the lack of progress they'd made. Nobody in the town seemed to know anything about the identity of the bandits including the town's magistrate, which Jacob found very suspicious but he kept that opinion to himself.

"It was gone three in the afternoon and the summer's sun was beating through the study's windows when Carp finally asked where Alfie Bicks was. It was something that had been concerning Jacob since the meeting had begun, his tall bodyguard had spent the morning interrogating the landing crew from the previous evening. Jacob wondered if Alfie had managed to discover too much and had been silenced for his troubles, he certainly hoped not.

"Another hour passed by before a loud thud was heard on the front door of Bates' headquarters, silencing the study. Jacob quickly signalled for several of his men to go and check it out. A moment later the room broke into chaos as Alfie Bicks was carried into the room covered in blood. The table was cleared and Alfie was laid down.

"Jacob Swift stood speechless as anger welled up inside him. His tall bodyguard and close friend who had watched his back since the first day Jacob had begun smuggling was barely conscious, his face was cut open and blood had soaked into his normally bushy beard whilst both of his eyes were virtually swollen shut.

"'Go get a doctor,' Carp ordered several of his men who wasted no time vanishing from the room. Thomas had moved to Alfie's side and was gently gripping his hand

"'Alfie who did this to you?' he kept repeating over and over. Alfie was struggling to keep conscious, eventually he managed to open his mouth slightly and Thomas lent towards his old friend putting his ear close to Alfie's mouth

"'The Jenkins B... B... Big Ronnie's back,' Alfie managed to mumble. Thomas' expression of anger vanished for a fraction of a second replaced by one of confusion.

"'Big Ronnie Jenkins was banished more than a decade ago. It can't be true,' Thomas said looking in Jacob's direction for an answer but it was Alfie who managed to deliver it just before he slipped under once again. 'H... He earned his freedom an g... got back here on a ship,' was all Alfie Bicks could manage."

Chapter 24

"For the rest of that day Billy Bates' old headquarters perched high up on the chalk cliffs was a hive of activity; war had officially been declared. Jacob Swift now knew the danger he faced and was willing to take no chances, he ordered a handful of his men to make their way to his townhouse and pick up his father who was vulnerable and too easy a target for the Jenkins crew who wouldn't hesitate slaying an innocent man to get to the leader of Billy Bates' old organisation.

"Jacob was far from stupid, he knew Big Ronnie and his clan only wanted one thing... money and The Boy wasn't prepared to part with a single penny.

"The order was given to his back row to gather the troops and within an hour fifty men had arrived at the headquarters. It was located in a remote area with good views in every direction. Bill had chosen the house for that very reason. With fifty armed men at Jacob's side the house was impossible to penetrate. Jacob knew the Jenkins would have to be suicidal to attack him there.

"A doctor had eventually arrived and began to work on Alfie who was in a really bad way. Jacob prayed that his tall bodyguard would make it, but he knew it was touch and go. When the sun began to drop out of the summer sky Jacob gathered his back row for a meeting in the study. That night three cargoes were being landed on the beach. In the end The Boy decided to dispatch thirty men armed with rifles and muskets to watch over the operations and make sure that his merchandise made it to the safe houses where it was stored.

Jacob had received orders for his cargoes and, when you placed an order with The Boy, he always delivered; he'd worked hard to establish a good reputation as someone whose word was worth something and he wasn't prepared to have it ruined for the sake of a gang of thugs like the Jenkins family.

He also needed a steady flow of goods to keep his supply of money flowing, if the money ran dry so would some of his men's loyalty as doubts would enter their minds about whether their young boss was up to the task of running such a large operation. Some would inevitably try and jump ship before it sank whilst others would stand by his side no matter what, he was sure of that.

"Thankfully though, that evening nobody attacked the landing crews, whether it was down to his show of force or just blind luck it came as a relief to Jacob. He spent that evening surrounded by his father and most trusted friends staring into the flames of Bill's old log fire and pondering what the great man would have done if he'd found himself in the same situation. Jacob could almost hear Bill's croaky voice, 'Remember attack is often the best form of defence', the old rogue had said more than once to his young apprentice. It was those words that stuck in Jacob's mind and, as he watched the flames, they echoed through his thoughts.

"From what Jacob had learnt about Ronnie Jenkins, he knew the huge man was an equally huge problem and it wasn't going to go away until blood was shed. Looking over at Thomas, Jacob knew that bloodshed was unavoidable now anyway, even if the Jenkins gave up and left town, Thomas would hunt them down. The squat bodyguard who'd barely said more than a few words since Bill's death spent most of that evening alone with Alfie gripping the tall man's hand and whispering promises of revenge into his ear.

"When the day broke Jacob awoke and made his way to the kitchen stepping over at least a dozen of his men who were scattered everywhere sleeping, many had been up most of the night on guard duty so The Boy left them to it, they certainly deserved some sleep. It wasn't long though before everybody was up and about drinking tea and smoking their pipes whilst they washed the remnants of sleep away.

"Jacob Swift had a general idea of what he was going to do about the Jenkins crew; he didn't like it, it was far too risky but they didn't have enough information and he had to do something. Thankfully, his risky plan went straight out of the window when one of Carp's men who'd been in the town trying to gather information turned up at the headquarters with a young boy of twelve or so. It was Carp's man who entered the room first leaving the kid outside, the man looked shattered he'd been working hard on Jacob's behalf but still managed to wish both Carp and Jacob good morning before he got to the point. 'This lad came up to me in the town, said he'd heard that I work for Jacob Swift who he had a message for, the cheeky little mite wouldn't give it up, boss, even when I threatened him. He said he needed to deliver it in person.'

"Jacob thought about this for a moment before he looked up at Carp's man. 'You frisk him?' he asked.

"'Of course,' the man replied, to which Jacob asked the man to show him in. A moment later a young boy entered the room, he was dressed in rags or what Jacob had come to think of as rags, years ago he'd called them clothes. The young boy also had mud and grime smeared up his face and forearms but he stood in front of Jacob with a look of pride on his face.

"'And you are?' Jacob asked the young man who was staring at The Boy with a twinkle in his eyes.

"'My name's Charlie, Sir,' he said, Jacob smiled but didn't bother correcting the young boy for calling him 'Sir' like Billy Bates had done to him years before. Jacob's life had gone full circle in the short years he'd been around.

"'Pleased to meet you, Charlie,' Jacob said extending his hand to which the young boy stepped forward and shook with a beaming smile plastered on his muddy face.

"'I hear you have a message for me?' Jacob asked; the boy nodded.

"'I heard your men were asking around about any suspicious men in the area,' Jacob's ears pricked up and young Charlie had his full attention.

"'Yeah they were, what do you know?' Jacob asked the young man who looked down at the floor nervously 'don't worry, Charlie,' Jacob reassured him.

"Finally young Charlie looked up at Jacob. 'Well sometimes, Sir, I have to poach on Lord Northbourne's estate. I never take more than we can eat,' he said, Jacob smiled, he couldn't care less about some rich lord's pheasants.

"'Well, there's been some activity up in the woods there, a big gang of men, thirty or so on horseback sleeping rough. I thought you'd want to know, Mr. Swift,' the young boy said with no idea how priceless the information he'd just delivered was to Jacob Swift, who suddenly had enough information to form a plan that had a chance of success. Jacob sat back in his chair and relaxed as a broad smile crossed his youthful face. He turned to Carp who was nodding slowly. It was music to their ears.

"'Go gather the back row for a meeting in ten minutes,' he said to Carp who quickly shuffled out of the room leaving Jacob alone with the young man.

"'Charlie. Why exactly were you so determined to tell me that in person? You put yourself in danger coming here, you understand that, don't you?' Jacob said, he was still a little suspicious of a trap but he could see the young man in front of him was completely genuine. Young Charlie fell silent for a moment and once again glanced down at the floor; for the first time since he'd entered the study he looked embarrassed.

"'I wanted to meet you, Mr. Swift,' he finally said. 'You're a hero, they say you were born poor like me and now you're the richest and most powerful man in this town.'

"The study fell silent for a moment as young Charlie's words found their mark. Jacob spent a lot of time mixing with the wealthy and powerful. Men and women who'd been born into money and provided with the best of everything from birth. He wasn't one of them he knew that much, they knew it too but, like Bill, had said, 'always know the difference between fear and respect'. Deep down Jacob Swift had much more in common with the young boy dressed in rags in front of his eyes.

"He rose to his feet and walked over to the boy who was still staring down at the floor. Jacob knelt down so they were at eye level and young Charlie looked up at him. He gripped the boy's hand and opened his palm where he placed more money than most men would earn in a year. Young Charlie let out a faint gasp, as he looked down at the money speechless .

124

"'You know a farm called Prosperity on the outskirts of town?' Jacob asked young Charlie who was still a little shocked but managed to nod. 'There's a farmer there called Havelock,' Jacob continued. 'You go see him and tell him I sent you, I'm sure he'll have some work for you.'

"Young Charlie had a smile on his face as he strolled out of the study passing Thomas' squat frame in the doorway. Jacob glanced at his bodyguard whose sombre face showed little emotion. 'Gather the troops,' Jacob ordered."

Chapter 25

"The study where Bill had begun Jacob's apprenticeship years before was crammed packed when the meeting finally began. The Boy's back row, his most trusted batmen, enforcers, landers and his inner circle of advisers had gathered to discuss what they'd learnt from the young poacher, Charlie, and how best to proceed. Jacob knew he had some hard decisions to make, choices he'd have to live with for the rest of his life.

"Thomas was eager to launch a full-scale attack, Jacob's tough and loyal bodyguard's judgment was clouded by anger and he was unable to even consider the consequences of the action he was keen to take.

"'Let's wipe Ronnie and his clan off the map, once and for all,' he roared at the table before looking at Jacob for the approval he needed. Jacob Swift had far more control though. Giving the order for an attack on the scale Thomas demanded was a big decision and one that Jacob needed time to think over.

"'Calm down, you'll get your revenge, my brother, don't worry,' The Boy promised Thomas who took some deep breaths. The man was suffering that was clear for everyone to see. Thomas needed to release his anger in an explosion of violence and Jacob knew he could only restrain the man for so long.

"The Boy glanced slowly around the room at his men, at Jim Robson who was keen to prove his worth and establish a reputation, then at Carp the most skilled of all his men when it came to landing goods, eventually Jacob's eyes settled on a slim man with short cropped brown hair and spectacles. His name was Hester and, unlike most of Jacob's crew, he was smartly dressed.

"Hester had been working for Jacob for only a year but The Boy valued him greatly. Hester worked alongside Jacob organizing the countless deals and financial transactions The Boy made, he was a brilliant mathematician. He helped plan what to bring into the country, which of Jacob's many teams would take delivery, where the merchandise would be stored and, of course, where it would be sold. The mathematician worked alongside many of Jacob's crooked merchants taking orders and maximizing Jacob's profits with incredible efficiency.

"Jacob Swift was very happy to hear that the Jenkins family were camping out in the woodland on Lord Northbourne's estate but it wasn't enough. 'Listen, all we have at the moment is the word of a twelve-year-old poacher,' he warned his men who all nodded their agreement fearful of a trap. 'We need to send some lookouts,' The Boy continued, 'to check things out and make sure it actually is the Jenkins and that the whole clan's there.'

"'Here here,' Carp chipped in. 'If we do attack we need to get them all in one go.'

"The room fell silent at Carp's words as every man thought about the action they were about to take. Surprisingly, it was Hester who was the next to speak; the well-dressed man rose to his feet and addressed the room for the first time. Hester was in his mid-forties and had been living in the town his entire life, like Alfie Bicks, Thomas and even Carp, Hester could also remember Big Ronnie Jenkins from his heyday when the huge man had stabbed a sailor to death in broad daylight ending the Jenkins reign of terror.

"'Jacob, I just want to make sure you know that if you attack Ronnie's family and he manages to escape you'll be looking over your shoulder until the day you die and, from what I can remember of Big Ronnie, you won't have long to wait.' Hester warned his young boss. As Jacob thought about the hard choices he had to make he could see his men waiting for their orders. Out of the corner of his eye he watched Thomas gritting his teeth, the man wanted Big Ronnie's blood and patience wasn't his strongest suit.

"He finally said. 'Thomas take twenty men out there on horseback. Tether them at Northbourne and make the rest of the journey on foot we don't want to tip them off. We don't attack yet, alright?' he ordered staring at his men before turning and looking over at Thomas and staring into his cold eyes. 'Understand?' he repeated.

"Thomas sighed before muttering, 'Yes,' under his breath.

"'I want to know how many are out there, count the horses too and when you ride back leave five armed men to keep lookout,' Jacob continued. 'And don't get seen at all costs.'

"The Boy watched every man at the table agree with the plan. He saw displeasure on several of their faces. Nobody was looking forward to what they were being forced to do but they had little choice. Of course there was one exception Jacob reminded himself as he glanced over at Thomas who was already making preparations with his men.

"A short time later, the squat bodyguard left Bill's old headquarters with his small army and Jacob prayed that Thomas would resist the temptation from the demons haunting him and encouraging him to extract his revenge, for his long-time friend Alfie Bicks but, above anything else, for Billy Bates' death.

"Carp left too with several of his men, not on a scouting mission but down into the town to visit some of his informants. Jacob sat watching The Channel and the many different ships through the study's bay windows like he had on hundreds of occasions. All The Boy could do was wait, hope and, of course, pray.

*

"Several slow and painful hours passed until somebody arrived back at Bates' old headquarters, they were seen by The Boy's armed lookouts from a fair distance away and it was obvious that something had gone terribly wrong by the way they galloped up the track towards Bates' old house. But it wasn't Thomas or any of his men who'd ventured out to the woods, it was Carp and Jacob had never seen the man looking so scared in his life.

"He jumped from the saddle of his horse and ran up to the

balcony where Jacob stood with Jim Robson. He tried to talk but no words came out, he was breathless from the journey and needed a minute to compose himself. Whilst Carp puffed and panted trying to catch his breath Jacob glanced at Jim who returned the concerned look. Finally Carp looked up at Jacob. 'We've got big problems. I've just had a run in with Big Ronnie and half a dozen of his crew, they're in the town acting like they own it.' Carp said looking as white as a sheet.

"'Damn,' Jacob muttered as he racked his brain.

"'And I'm afraid it gets worse,' Carp continued, looking at his young employer through troubled eyes. 'They are holding two of my men captive, Ronnie wants a sit down to negotiate terms he says you have until four o-clock.'

"Jacob pulled out his pocket watch. It was nearly three. 'Where?' he asked.

"'The Ship Tavern, he told me to tell you that the magistrate's gonna be there so don't dare try it on and he also promises you'll be safe,' Carp said.

"'Safe,' Jacob huffed. 'What's Ronnie doing with that dog Rawlings?' he asked but he knew the answer, the magistrate was as crooked as they came.

"'Ronnie says if you don't show he's gonna kill my men then burn down your townhouse,' Carp warned. Jacob shook his head and exhaled loudly; he took a few steps forward and stared out at sea whilst he thought hard. He'd have to go he had no choice, but, without serious backup, he was taking a huge risk. Ronnie was an animal and Jacob doubted the huge man would restrain himself for the sake of the magistrate. With Alfie on his deathbed and most of his men including Thomas out on the scouting mission Jacob was put in a difficult position. The Boy knew that Jim Robson wouldn't let him down but his old school friend lacked both the reputation and experience Jacob needed right now. A moment later The Boy snapped into action, he'd had enough of hiding out at Bates' old headquarters, it was his town now and it was time everyone knew it.

"He glanced at Jim. 'Gather ten good men, we're leaving in twenty minutes,' he ordered and for a moment he continued to stare out at the sea praying that his bodyguard, Thomas, hadn't succumbed to his weakness and already launched an attack."

Chapter 26

"Jacob Swift and his gang made their way towards The Ship Tavern through the town's cobbled streets watching as mothers came out of their doors and grabbed their children hastily dragging them indoors. The street traders frantically packed their stalls away eager to get off the streets and avoid the troubles ahead. The town was alive with rumours that The Boy's grip on the area had been challenged. There was an eerie silence to the normally busy streets; the only noise Jacob could hear came from the clatter of horses' hooves as he made his way to his meeting with destiny. The Boy wasn't scared, though, and was keen to look Ronnie Jenkins in the eye and let the huge man know it.

"As they approached the tavern, Jacob could see several of the Jenkins' clan loitering outside the pub waiting for his arrival, the men looked sinister under the dim beam of the pub's lantern illuminating the doorway. They stared Jacob's way as he climbed from his horse and let one of his men tether her, then Jacob stared back with a smile on his face knowing that even they feared their unpredictable leader. Taking a deep breath, Jacob glanced around the street before he strolled into the tavern with Jim Robson and several others at his side.

"The tavern was normally a rough place to be, packed with sailors from a dozen ships anchored in the downs. Fights broke out regularly. Tonight though the place was virtually empty apart from a handful of men gathered around a table in the corner. As he strolled in, everyone looked his way and he spotted Big Ronnie immediately, the man was built like a shire horse but much uglier. He continued to stare Jacob's way as The Boy strolled over and sat opposite him at the table where he returned the stare. For several long and painful moments nobody said a thing. The two leaders who couldn't have looked more different stared each other down whilst their bodyguards flashed evil looks at each other from across the table. You could have cut the tension with a knife.

"Jacob had no doubts why people feared Ronnie Jenkins, the man looked like he belonged in a circus freak show, but Jacob always had the gift of hiding his true feelings and he even managed to smile at the big man who was beginning to look puzzled. Then Jacob looked over at the magistrate who was squeezed so tightly into a wooden chair it looked like it was going to explode under his bulbous weight, the corrupt lawman continued to sip his brandy with a smug grin plastered all over his face.

"'Magistrate Rawlings, always a great pleasure,' Jacob said and for a moment the smile left Jacob's face, then he looked back at Big Ronnie and with all his will he forced it to return.

"Finally the huge man spoke, 'I'm gonna keep this as short as possible, right.' Jacob nodded, eager to get the meeting over with.

"'You know when I heard that Bill had left his operation to a lad your age I thought he'd finally lost his marbles, but I've been learning a lot about you these last few days and I've got to admit I don't think he went crazy after all,' Ronnie said, as he stared into Jacob's eyes and studied the young man's reactions. 'You're running more loads than Bill ever did,' Ronnie said pausing as he looked down at his glass of brandy, Jacob watched a smile creep up on his face before he glanced up and into Jacob's eyes. 'But you wouldn't last five minutes in this game if you didn't have Alfie or that nutcase Bill took in off the streets at your side, you know that, don't you?' Ronnie asked looking at Jacob for the reply he expected, Jacob laughed slightly before he looked up at Ronnie.

"'Yeah, where are they now?' he said confidently as he looked to his side where Jim stood staring at Big Ronnie with contempt in his eyes. Ronnie gritted his teeth in anger and exhaled a lungful of air.

"'How is Alfie, anyway? Did he pull through?' Ronnie asked, watching Jacob and smiling at his reaction. 'And I hear that nutcase Thomas is still kicking about.' Ronnie paused as he looked up at the ceiling. 'You know,' he finally said. 'I'd a killed Bill a long time ago if it hadn't been for him, it proved to be a smart move on Bill's part taking him in like that, fathering him. But Thomas, he isn't right in the head, but I'm sure you know that by now,' Ronnie reflected, and then the giant's demeanour changed in an instant. 'Anyway enough with the pleasantries, I've wasted far too much time in the last decade just getting back here so this is how it's gonna work,' Ronnie spat out, his attitude had changed completely and he'd lost what little composure he'd managed to muster. 'You're gonna continue running your smuggling operations, it's clear you're good at it and let's face it most of the people you do business with wouldn't deal with a man like me, but from now on you pay us Jenkins £200 on the first Saturday of every month, we'll ride into town and pick up what's owed. The first instalments due tomorrow and once its paid I promise me and my clan will be gone,' Ronnie said.

"Jacob Swift nodded smiling as he thought about Ronnie's ludicrous offer, two hundred a month was an absolute fortune and would leave him and his men with a pittance. 'And what if I refuse?' Jacob asked looking at Ronnie without fear in his eyes which was something the leader of the Jenkins clan wasn't used to.

"Ronnie smiled. 'You know you've got some guts lad I give you that but I promise you'll beg me for forgiveness when I make you watch me butcher your father in front of your eyes,' the huge man said with no emotion whatsoever. Jacob looked into Ronnie's eyes and could see that it was no hollow threat. The man thought nothing of taking someone's life. Jacob himself had now lost his composure, the games were over and the fake smile had disappeared from the young man's face. 'Either way, I ride out of this town tomorrow; you get to choose whether or not I kill some of your friends before I leave, but don't worry I'll be back and I'll never go away,' Ronnie said and Jacob didn't doubt him for a moment.

"Out of the corner of Jacob's eye he could see Jim Robson struggling to restrain himself, a moment later Big Ronnie had noticed it too and was staring at Jim. What happened next came from nowhere and escalated in seconds.

"'You got a problem, tough man?' Ronnie spat in Jim's direction, instantly the several members of the Jenkins clan who were stood around the table reached into their jackets. Jim Robson stood his ground staring hard into Big Ronnie's eyes. In a second Big Ronnie Jenkins climbed to his feet, the huge man had to duck to avoid hitting his head on the ceiling. He towered over Jim whose bravery was very noble but Jacob's friend was no match for Ronnie's huge stature.

"In an instant Ronnie had lashed out with one of his huge fists sending Jim crashing to the tavern's floorboards, then he spun around and grabbed Jacob by the scruff of the neck lifting him several feet off the ground so their faces were only inches apart. 'You've got twenty-four hours to gather the first instalment, when your time's up we'll come looking,' he roared 'Now get out,' he said throwing Jacob to the floor where he crashed into a table and some chairs. Big Ronnie stood leering menacingly at Jacob as he walked out of the tavern defeated with his men who were propping up Jim Robson.

"The Boy swallowed his pride as he climbed onto his horse, he'd struggled coming to terms with the decision he knew he had to make, but now he'd met Big Ronnie he had no qualms about giving the order, nobody threatened his father's life. It was time to let Thomas off his leash and wipe the Jenkins family off the face of the earth once and for all."

Chapter 27

"Jacob Swift stood watching from several hundred yards away as his men surrounded the woods where the Jenkins family camped out. He was uncomfortable with the choice he'd had to make but the Jenkins had arrived in the town threatening him with few other options. It was gone three in the morning when he received the signal that his men were in place and ready to carry out the attack, all but Thomas who had chosen to tread a different path that night. Jacob's squat bodyguard had a lust for an entirely different target.

"For the briefest of moments, The Boy debated about giving his men the order, he knew even then that it was going to be something he would have on his conscience for the rest of his life. When he'd left the tavern humiliated only a few hours earlier The Boy had wasted no time gathering his troops. Thomas and his men had returned from their scouting mission with good news, indeed it was the Jenkins clan camping out on Lord Northbourne's estate. Thomas was eager to get blood on his hands and the Lord was out of town at present on a hunt himself leaving no witnesses.

"Jacob's trusted bodyguard was infuriated that Big Ronnie Jenkins had the audacity to threaten his boss' life and he swore to Jacob that he'd make the man pay. The Boy knew he was asking a lot of his men, smuggling was crossing the line with the law but with murder there was no going back. If anyone was caught they'd face the noose without a doubt. So, in a moving speech, the young leader gave them all the opportunity to turn around and return to their families. After all, it was only their livelihoods that had been threatened, for Jacob Swift it had been his life and even worse than that the life of his father. But that evening, along with his entire back row, all of The Boy's men stood their ground, not a single man left Bates' headquarters. Over the years Jacob had given them all work

135

when they'd needed it. He'd fed their families and provided warmth and shelter for the people they loved. His men weren't angels but not a single person of the fifty or so misfits gathered in front of Jacob was willing to leave his side in his moment of need and he felt incredibly proud.

"So, that night, as he stared into the dense woodland in the distance he knew the moment for hesitation had passed, glancing at Jim Robson who stood clutching a rifle only a few metres away Jacob Swift spoke the words that would haunt his soul for years to come 'Attack,' he ordered. Within moments his men were pouring into the woods and disappearing past the tree line. They'd caught their enemies off guard that was clear enough as the flashes of gunshot lit up the sky followed by explosions that echoed through the night. Jacob felt a stab of pain in his guts as the last drop of his innocence bled out of him, The Boy hadn't fired a single shot but he was in charge of the men who had.

"After around five minutes or so, the gunshots finally ceased returning some peace to the summer night. Jacob's mind drifted to his troubled friend, Thomas, and he hoped with all his heart that his bodyguard had been as successful with his own attack on the Jenkins clan's leader Big Ronnie. The giant of a man was staying over in one of the town's inns with several of his men as backup.

"For Jacob it had been the most difficult week of his entire life, beginning with the death of his mentor, Billy Bates, and ending with a massacre. 'Would things ever return to normal after this?' Jacob asked himself. He certainly hoped so but, unknown to the young leader, things were going to get worse before they got better and even more trouble lay ahead.

*

"The town's network of winding cobbled streets were empty with everyone fast asleep locked safely away in their houses when Thomas and two of his most ruthless men made their way in silence towards the inn where Big Ronnie Jenkins was hiding out. The leader of the Jenkins family had taken several of his clan with him into the town for protection, but as Thomas checked the weapons he carried he was confident Ronnie's bodyguards would fail their task. Thomas had grown up on the streets and he was more than capable even with his huge size of moving around unseen, it had been one of the many tricks he'd learnt that had kept him alive until Bill had taken him in.

"Thomas forced the painful memories of Bill from his mind temporarily; he couldn't afford to be distracted. Signalling for his men to watch over the Inn's entrance and exit, Thomas made his way around to the rear of the building. With absolute focus Jacob's bodyguard quickly forced open the door making very little noise.

"Entering the building, he crept through a passageway leading to the Inn's lobby. As predicted, one of Ronnie's men was seated on a stool, keeping a close eye on the Inn's front doorway. Using the lantern's dim light to his advantage Thomas crept behind the man silencing him with a razor to his throat. The man's last words were whispered pleas revealing his leader's room number in the hope that Thomas would show some mercy, which was something the man was incapable of. Moments later Thomas had made his way through the building and had entered Big Ronnie's room, he kept his eyes constantly trained on the huge man spread out on the bed.

"Thomas hadn't seen Ronnie in over a decade but he wouldn't ever have forgotten the man's rugged face. Whilst he stood watching Big Ronnie breathe in and out in the fits of sleep Thomas debated about ending the man's life right there and then. In the end he decided that wouldn't quite satisfy his lust for revenge. Thomas needed to look into Big Ronnie's eyes when he took the man's life. Ronnie Jenkins had threatened Bill a long time ago and, for that offence alone, the man would die slowly.

"Fiddling in the dark with some matches, Thomas lit a lantern which spread a dim light across the room. He stood watching as Ronnie stirred and eventually opened his eyes. The man knew something was wrong immediately and his eyes fell on the figure stood in the shadows like the grim reaper

137

ready to claim what he was owed.

"Snarling like an animal Big Ronnie climbed to his feet where he towered over Thomas ready to take the man on. Thomas took a step forward out of the shadows revealing his identity and for the first time since Bill's body had been found the man actually smiled as he pulled an axe from his jacket. Now the snarl had disappeared from Big Ronnie's face and for the first time in his life he was paralyzed with fear as Thomas raised the axe and swung it in his direction.

*

"Like every day of that eventful week, the following would stick in Jacob's mind until the day he died. He would ponder what would have happened if he had dealt with things differently knowing that it was too late to do anything about it. That week had changed everything for Jacob Swift and the young man managed to burn all the bridges he'd spent years building with one throw of the dice.

"Big Ronnie's body was found early the next morning. The huge man had been hacked into several pieces that were spread across the room where he'd been staying. The floor along with most of the walls and even the ceiling were flecked in the man's blood. It was the most gruesome murder in the town's history and, even in the last 200 years, nobody's even come close to matching it.

"His bodyguard, one of Ronnie's younger brothers, was found in the Inn's reception area, Thomas had shown a little mercy after all in comparison and had only sliced the man's throat killing him very quickly.

"Like all of Jacob's men who were involved in the events of that fateful night, The Boy hadn't slept, he now knew a storm really was coming his way. News of Big Ronnie's death spread through the town's streets that morning, to most of the locals it came as a relief. The Jenkins family had few friends in the area, they were known generally as a menace. That being said, Ronnie's death was the most horrific thing anybody in the town had ever seen and it didn't take much for people to figure out who was responsible. Thomas had sent a chilling message not to mess with The Boy and everyone took note.

"It was on that eventful morning that people's opinions of Jacob Swift began to change, he'd been known as a polite young man who'd help anyone in need. People's views swung from respect for him to fearing him and from that day on they viewed him like they viewed his mentor, the man who had unknowingly started that week's disastrous chain of events... Billy Bates."

Chapter 28

"Jacob arrived back at Bill's old headquarters at nine the following morning and was greeted by Thomas, who, unlike everybody else, seemed unfazed by the morning's events. The pair talked at length about how their plans had unfolded and Jacob was pleased to hear that Big Ronnie Jenkins would no longer cause a threat to his life and that of his father's. Thomas didn't go into graphic detail about how the ruthless leader had begged for his life in his last moments on this earth.

"Whilst Jacob, Thomas and a handful of men ate a hearty breakfast, several miles away others were still hard at work digging a deep pit in the tough chalky ground beneath the woodland on Lord Northbourne's estate. When they finally finished Jacob's gang of smuggling misfits laid down their picks and shovels beginning the task of hauling the countless bodies of the Jenkins clan into the pit where they'd stay undiscovered until the end of time, or so young Jacob Swift thought. Eventually the pit was filled in and the ground covered over with a layer of dead leaves to hide where the ground had been disturbed.

"That morning, when Jacob's men left the woodland, the summer sun was high in the sky; all traces of the Jenkins family were gone, hidden deep under the ground. Unlike their leader Big Ronnie whose death was about to become a very public affair, his family's was a closely-guarded secret that Jacob's men would take to their graves. Every man present that night had been sworn to secrecy by Jacob himself. It was forbidden to even mention the attack on Lord Northbourne's grounds and any man found to have loose lips faced the consequences of being silenced by The Boy's right hand man Thomas, a fate that scared most men more than the noose itself.

"That morning, though, before they'd even left the

woodland and began making their way towards the coast, soldiers had already arrived in the town, marching through the narrow cobbled streets. The corrupt magistrate, Theodore Rawlings, who over time had earned a pretty penny out of The Boy, Jacob Swift, and whose greed had led him to eventually betray him was called for as soon as Ronnie Jenkins' body had been found. When Rawlings had entered the small inn where the murder had taken place he was unfazed, the magistrate had presided over countless murders during his long career but when he came across the body of Big Ronnie, the magistrate turned pale and then a moment later was physically sick. Theodore Rawlings was shocked to his corrupt core by the scene in front of his eyes. It was unnatural, the work of a devil. Whilst the magistrate stared at the brutal scene, he realised how wrong he'd been to betray Jacob Swift and instantly the magistrate began to fear for his own life.

"Jacob was very smart, he'd been taught by a man who'd survived countless wars with rival gangs and the law over the decades, Billy Bates had taught his apprentice well, Rawlings knew Jacob wouldn't attack the magistrate but The Boy wouldn't hesitate sending one of his lieutenants, Alfred Bicks if he'd managed to survive or even that animal, Thomas. Neither would hesitate carrying out their boss's orders; the scene in front of him told him that much. It wasn't until a dozen soldiers arrived from the local garrison that the magistrate breathed a sigh of relief.

"Realising that he'd made a huge enemy in young Jacob, the magistrate swore that he'd try and put things right, to save his own skin if nothing else. He knew he'd be safe whilst he was backed up by soldiers of the crown, but they wouldn't be around to watch his back forever and The Boy would pick his moment well. Theodore Rawlings knew he was in a difficult position, on the one hand he needed to bring a murderer to justice, and somebody would have to pay the price. The victim, Ronnie Jenkins, had threatened Jacob Swift in public which was something nobody had dared to do whilst Billy Bates still breathed, and had been found butchered only hours later. It didn't take a genius to figure out who was responsible. On the other hand, Rawlings knew he wouldn't survive until the end of the week if he went after Jacob for the crime. Theodore Rawlings was left with only one option he had to try and make a deal with The Boy, a deal that would mean Jacob sacrificing one of his own men. The magistrate hoped Jacob Swift would be smart enough to take it.

*

"Jacob's men were still on high alert at Bates' old headquarters that day and they wasted no time warning their young boss when they spotted the horse-drawn carriage making its way up the track towards the cliff-top house. Most of the men began to panic when they realised that the carriage not only belonged to the crooked magistrate but was flanked by several of the King's soldiers. Most had experienced their fair share of run-ins with Rawlings over the years and knew the man wasn't to be trusted. Jacob re-assured his men as the carriage approached the house, reminding them that the magistrate was only looking for one murderer and there was no real evidence. Thomas had made sure of that, the fearless bodyguard and enforcer of Jacob's vast smuggling empire had been trained to kill at a very young age and was ruthlessly efficient.

"When the carriage finally pulled to a stop outside the house, tension was high, a dozen of Jacob's men stood scattered around staring in silence as the carriage doors opened and the magistrate climbed out looking as tired as The Boy himself who hadn't slept properly in days.

"'Magistrate Rawlings, to what do I owe this pleasure?' Jacob asked with a fake smile plastered across his youthful face whilst he stared at the magistrate's reactions eager to know how much the man knew. The magistrate failed to return the smile or even hide his surprise at Jacob's pleasant greeting. He stepped forward and approached The Boy whilst he glanced both ways aware of the countless eyes staring in his direction. What the Magistrate was about to say were for Jacob Swift's ears only.

"'Listen Jacob, I admit this is a complete mess we've found ourselves in.'

"'What do you mean?' Jacob asked. The magistrate shook his head and looked down at the ground before he glanced up and looked straight into Jacob's eyes.

"'Don't play games with me, we both know why I'm here,' he growled at Jacob who stared at him for a long moment before either man spoke. 'I know you've little reason to trust me, Jacob, but, believe it or not, I'm here to help you; it isn't too late to come to a solution that benefits us both,' Rawlings said firmly, Jacob stared at him in disbelief as anger rose within him.

"'What! Don't tell me you have the audacity to ask for more money,' he spat out losing his cool. The magistrate glanced in either direction making sure the soldiers who were tending to their horses were out of earshot.

"'Jacob, the only thing I need right now is someone to hang for Ronnie's murder, there's no other option, murder's murder someone has to pay the price,' Rawlings pleaded.

"Jacob was deep in thought, he took a moment to answer, suspicious of a trap, 'And what does this have to do with me?' he finally asked.

"The magistrate took a deep breath and looked Jacob Swift in the eye. 'You need to give up one of your men; let them take the fall, in time this whole episode will blow over,' he barely whispered.

"Jacob exhaled a lungful of air genuinely shocked at the magistrate's words, a moment later he had composed himself. 'I could never do that, unlike you I understand the meaning of loyalty,' he replied through gritted teeth. Rawlings shook his head, he was taking a risk trying to help Jacob but the young man couldn't see it. The magistrate was hoping Jacob would co-operate for both their sakes. He tried one last time to convince The Boy there was no other option but he wouldn't hear it. Whilst the magistrate climbed back into his coach he warned Jacob one last time, 'Somebody has to pay, can't you see that?' he pleaded but The Boy refused to listen, which was something else he'd live to regret.

*

"That night Jacob retired to bed early, it had been a strenuous week and he was near exhaustion when his head hit the pillow, within moments he fell into a deep sleep but at midnight he was woken by Thomas. The squat bodyguard stood at the door of Bill's old bedroom with a look of grave concern on his normally emotionless face. Jacob was up instantly sensing that something was amiss and he wasn't wrong. Earlier that evening Jim Robson had left Bill's headquarters and ventured into the town. He was courting a young lady whom he'd arranged to meet. Unlike Jacob who was very shy and reserved whilst around the opposite sex, Jim was a ladies' man. He had built a tough reputation in the town and was known to be very close to Jacob Swift. On top of that he had cash to boot too which was something that always attracted women. That evening Jim had planned to move unseen wearing a hooded cloak to avoid being spotted, he knew the risks but young Jim hadn't managed to meet up with his lady friend after all. A few minutes before Thomas had woken Jacob a messenger had arrived at the cliff-top house bringing devastating news.

"Jacob's old school friend had been recognized by none other than Theodore Rawlings himself, immediately Jim had been set on by a handful of soldiers. He was arrested on the spot and formally charged with the cold blooded murder of Ronald Jenkins.

"As Thomas informed his young boss of the tragic turn of events Jacob could clearly see the huge man felt terribly for his friend and ultimately responsible for the charges that had been brought against him. Jacob's brain was racing and reaching no positive conclusions. 'So what's going to happen to him?' he finally asked.

"Thomas looked down at the floor whilst he replied, 'He's going to be hanged in two days' time on market day in Alfred Square,' he said weakly. Jacob was speechless and found himself burying his head in his hands."

Chapter 29

Reg Cooper stopped telling his story and glanced over at young Stanley who was seated next to him looking deep in thought. The old curator smiled as he reached for the flask on the desk in front of him.

"I think it's time for that coffee, don't you?" he asked. Stan nodded before he looked around the museum that was stuffed with odd-looking artefacts and only lacked one important thing... visitors.

A moment later, he was on his feet wandering around the exhibits whilst Reg Cooper sat in silence sipping his coffee watching young Stan with curiosity. Eventually the young man stopped strolling and stood staring up at an old ship's figurehead of a beautiful lady carved from oak. Reg knew the identity of the lady, he also knew the figurehead had never been fastened to the ship it had been made for; it still held its original paint that had flaked and worn away in places. Reg chuckled to himself as he watched Stanley. 'Of all the exhibits in the museum, he pays special attention to that one,' the old man thought, 'was it a coincidence? Or had destiny brought young Stan to the museum in the first place?' Reg Cooper was beginning to think so.

Suddenly Stan glanced over at Reg as if he'd read the old man's thoughts. "Reg there's a date carved in here," he shouted as he traced over the numbers on the base of the figurine with his fingers. "1792... Wow," he said excitedly as he turned to the museum's curator who had a huge smile on his face. Watching Stanley's enthusiasm made him feel happier than he had in years.

"She's pretty, isn't she?" Reg called out from the other side of the museum where he was still drinking his coffee.

Stan stared up at the lady's face. "She's beautiful," he replied as he gazed in amazement, too transfixed on the figurehead to witness Reg Cooper wipe a tear from the corner of his eye. A moment later Stan turned around and strolled back to the museum's reception where he sat back down in his seat. "So what happened to Jim Robson?" he asked, eager to learn whether Jacob Swift's friend managed to survive.

Reg laughed and shook his head. "Patience is a virtue, Stan. In time you'll find out everything about Jim Robson, but for now I do have something I can show you," Reg said as he slowly climbed to his feet and hobbled across to the other side of the museum where he stopped in front of a chest of drawers and fumbled in his pockets for a key. Eventually he opened a drawer and pulled out an old newspaper which he handed to Stan who stared down at the front page, it was dated the 28th June 1978 and was a copy of *The East Kent Reporter*, the town's local paper that was still in circulation.

The paper had faded brown over the years but its front page headline was still readable. "Oh, my god," Stan found himself mumbling; he glanced up at Reg who smiled warmly before he took another sip of his coffee and let Stan read the article.

When he'd finished Stan sat staring at it for a moment, trying to make sense of it all. He turned to Reg hesitant to ask the one question that was jumping out at him; in the end he couldn't resist.

"Reg, why didn't you tell everyone the truth? You knew exactly who the bodies belonged to but you kept that to yourself, why?" Stan asked. Reg Cooper thought for a long moment, pushing his spectacles up the bridge of his nose. "Why would you do that?" Stan demanded.

The old man nodded slowly. "I think it's time we continued the story," he said hoping that, in the end, Stan would understand why he'd kept his mouth shut back in the 1970s when they'd found the Jenkins family's final resting place.

The East K

Sunday, 25th June 1978

Mass grave found in woods

Local police, historians and forensic experts rushed to woodland in Northbourne last Friday when workmen fitting gas pipelines unearthed a mass grave.

The bodies, 29 in total and all male, were buried together in a deep pit and are believed to date back several hundred years. Experts believe that the men died in battle. Most of the bodies display injuries consistent with gunshot wounds and several samples of musket shot were found on the site. But what has shocked everyone alike is that testing carried out on the bodies has proven that the men were all closely related. Local historian Arthur Mackenzie is baffled by the find and has failed to find any reference to the incident in the areas history.

The bodies are assumed to be the result of a skirmish between local families in the late 18th century. Anyone who can shed some light on the mystery we'd like to encourage coming forward and contacting Kent police. Several artefacts were removed from the site and investigations continue.

Rer
foll
imp

The
that
rela
the
beh
of a
exp
in li
its
beh
con
or v

It m
tote
thir
dec
mos
rati

Chapter 30

"Market day soon came around. It was a day which normally brought most folk in the town out to the small square. On that particular day though the entire town had come out to see Jim Robson pay the price for Ronnie Jenkins' murder. The small cobbled square and even the streets leading to and from were packed with people everywhere. Stallholders sold their usual wares of fishing nets, glass jars, bottles, smoking pipes and such. Dead pigeons, rabbits and chickens hung from the beams above the stalls whilst wicker baskets full to the brim with fresh fish littered the ground. Farmers bartered over the sale of their livestock as young pickpockets roamed through the crowds earning a crust from the rich who'd ventured out to witness, with morbid curiosity, the hanging of one of Jacob Swift's top men.

"The town had been rife with rumours and speculation since Big Ronnie Jenkins' body had been found. The Boy himself hadn't been seen for days, but according to local gossip his cargoes were still hitting the shores. Some people were saying that Jacob had vanished since his friend's capture and was on the run from the law, whilst others were saying The Boy had been caught himself. It was a rumour that was certainly believable for the townsfolk who'd witnessed first-hand the build-up of the King's men in their streets over the past week.

"In the corner of the market square stood a wooden stage, its sole purpose was for handing out local punishment. Every week on market day thieves and bandits would be dragged on to the stage shackled, where they'd receive a flogging for their crime overseen by none other than the magistrate, Theodore Rawlings himself, backed up by a handful of soldiers from the town's garrison.

"On the day of Jim's execution, a dozen soldiers guarded

the stage with their guns drawn. Theodore Rawlings knew only too well how much power Jacob Swift wielded in the town. The locals held him in high regard, considered him a hero even. On that day tension was high and the magistrate was taking no chances. Jim Robson was well-known in the town and liked by most. He was polite, a quality Jacob encouraged amongst his men, but handy with his fists when he needed to be. He was no angel, but a cold-blooded murderer he was not. Rumours had spread the length and width of Jacob's territory about who in fact had spilled Big Ronnie's blood. People knew Jim Robson was a tough lad but they doubted whether he was capable of taking out Ronnie Jenkins, who was an all-out savage. Everyone in the town knew that Jacob's tall red-bearded, knife-wielding bodyguard had been beaten to within an inch of his life only days earlier, so that ruled Alfie Bicks out, who was certainly capable of murder. In the town's eyes that only left one suspect and it certainly wasn't the young man about to be executed.

"When Jim was led out, it took Theodore Rawlings several moments to silence the crowd who booed in disgust at the injustice about to be carried out. The magistrate sensed trouble was ahead and, fearing a riot, he wasted no time reading out the charges brought against Jim Robson. The crowd continued to boo even as Rawlings slipped the noose around Jim's thick neck. Jacob's old school friend was forced to climb up onto a stool in the centre of the stage before the rope was pulled tight and fastened. Jim stood with his muscular arms tied together behind his back. His bulk and strength were useless but his courage held firm as he stared into the crowd, recognising the faces of people he'd done business with over the years on Jacob Swift's behalf.

"In the last moments, as tension built up and the magistrate read out Jim's last rights, every man, woman and child in the crowd took a deep breath. Many looked down at the ground not willing to witness the injustice dealt out against young Jim. The entire market square that was normally bustling with noise became eerily quiet as Theodore Rawlings signalled for one of his men to kick away the stool.

"The soldier stepped forward and approached Jim but at the very last moment he stopped in his tracks, distracted by a growing noise at the back of the crowd. Everyone's eyes began to dart around as dozens of men carrying thick wooden bats and dressed in black with their faces covered began pouring into the small square from every entrance. Theodore Rawlings glanced at his soldiers who were staring with a look of panic on their faces at the scene unfolding in front of their eyes. Then, suddenly, the crowd began to part as the noise of horses' hooves on the cobbles filled the air.

"Jacob Swift appeared astride his pure white horse looking quite the picture as he casually trotted through the crowded square. Unlike his men's, The Boy's face wasn't covered. Jacob Swift had gone way past the point of reprisals from the law. The events of that week had turned him into a true outlaw. He'd burnt all his bridges and life wouldn't ever be the same for him, he knew he no longer had anything to lose.

"The crowd was dead silent as Jacob Swift approached the stage where his good friend was still bound and strung up balancing on the wooden stool. The soldiers were all levelling their guns directly at Jacob now but The Boy only smiled in response.

"'Jacob Swift, this is an outrage! Order your men from this square immediately or god help you, I have a dozen armed men,' Theodore Rawlings warned, looking red-faced and outraged. The crowd was silent as Jacob stared at Rawlings for a long moment.

"'Untie my friend now or every one of you will die today,' he finally shouted at the soldiers who were all glancing at each other, unaware of what to do, most had heard all about the notorious smuggler people called The Boy and knew he was a man of his word.

"Rawlings shook his head. 'Your men and their bats won't hold up against firepower,' the magistrate warned. Then Jacob Swift did something that scared Theodore Rawlings to the core, in a simple gesture The Boy laughed to himself then raised his left hand high in the air. Simultaneously dozens of rifle barrels appeared over the rooftops surrounding the entire square, all loaded and aimed in the magistrate's direction. Theodore Rawlings stood speechless as his soldiers put down their arms and raised their hands in surrender.

"Pulling a musket from his jacket Jacob levelled it straight at Rawlings. 'Now untie my friend or I'm going to kill you,' he stated, and the magistrate didn't doubt him for a second. Immediately Jim Robson was untied, he strolled towards Jacob grinning from ear to ear. Jacob extended his hand and hauled his friend up onto the back of his horse.

"There was a mixed reaction amongst the crowd, some stood speechless at what they'd seen but most cheered The Boy as he trotted out of the market square that day. Years later they'd retell the story, over and over, making Jacob Swift a legend in the town. But, on that day as he trotted away the barrels of the guns held by his men on the rooftops disappeared along with his batmen in the square, all traces of The Boy's presence disappeared as quickly as it had arrived, leaving the corrupt magistrate and his band of soldiers red-faced and humiliated.

*

"Later that same day when the sun had fallen out of the sky and the townsfolk had finally stopped recounting the tale of Jim's rescue so they could retire to bed, an old drunk staggered out of the Alehouse where he'd been boozing all day. Turning onto the track leading towards his house Henry Cutler, the man who'd helped Big Ronnie and his clan wage their short lived war against Jacob Swift began his stagger home.

"Cutler had been good friends with Ronnie back in the huge man's heyday, but that wasn't why he'd helped him, for Cutler it had all been about revenge on Bill's right hand man, Alfie Bicks. Cutler had never been able to extract his revenge on Bates for the scar he'd left on his face all those years ago, but Alfie Bicks was good enough. Cutler was a little disappointed to hear of Ronnie's death but when the old drunk had weighed it up he'd come to the conclusion that his revenge on Alfie had been worth it. Whilst he staggered home on the track, Henry Cutler pictured Alfie on the floor covered in his own blood and the feeling of satisfaction it had given him to put the boot in on his old enemy.

"Cutler was dragged from his thoughts as a lone figure stepped from some bushes beside the track. Cutler froze on the spot as the tall figure approached him, as he got closer Cutler could make out the silhouette of the man's beard. Finally Cutler began to plead as he recognized the bruised and swollen face, but more importantly the glint from the blade the man carried in his right hand. For Henry Cutler there was no mistaking it, his old enemy Alfie Bicks had pulled through after all."

Chapter 31

"After that day in the market square when Jim Robson was dramatically rescued from the noose, life changed for Jacob Swift. Smuggling was a crime but it was petty in comparison to threatening the King's men at gunpoint and freeing a suspected murderer, that was a different kettle of fish entirely and now The Boy attracted the attention of a great deal more lawmen than just Magistrate Rawlings.

"Up until that point in time, Jacob's smuggling empire had been the largest in the land. Over the years as he'd turned into a man The Boy had made the most of having the continent on his doorstep. He was able to arrange cargoes to land on his shores on a daily basis whilst other smugglers across the land would take days, weeks even to make the necessary arrangements. But Billy Bates' death had set in motion a chain of events that would make young Jacob a target not only for the Customs, excise men and the preventative force but for the soldiers of the Crown as well.

"Immediately on the day of Jims rescue, Theodore Rawlings had left the town's small square red-faced and humiliated but determined to bring young Jacob Swift to justice. As far as the magistrate was concerned, The Boy had really overstepped the mark. Rawlings knew if he went after Jacob he would need to take out both Alfie and Thomas; he knew either man would spill blood for their young leader.

"It took several days for a warrant to be drawn up for Jacob Swift's arrest but Rawlings didn't waste any time hitting Jacob where he knew it would hurt, along with a handful of soldiers he approached the small gang of preventative officers dispatched on our stretch of coast. The crooked magistrate used all his pull in the area to gather information about cargoes being landed on our shores, he threatened every snitch who owed him a favour and, when that didn't work, he used his own money to buy information. For Theodore Rawlings catching The Boy was no longer just business, his war with Jacob Swift was as personal as it got.

"Every piece of information about Jacob's gang that the magistrate got his greedy hands on he passed to the small band of preventative officers on land. For the first time they began successfully confiscating cargoes from smugglers who worked on Jacob Swift's behalf. Theodore Rawlings wasn't a stupid man, he knew this not only cost Jacob a pretty penny but it damaged his reputation, which up to that point had been impeccable. So began the game of cat and mouse between the crooked magistrate and the town's young smuggler, a pair that, once upon a time, had been happy to do business together.

"Thomas was keen to offer his services and silence Rawlings once and for all but Jacob knew better and knew it wasn't the right solution and would only bring more attention down on his smuggling empire. Billy Bates had spent years picking his successor and had chosen Jacob Swift wisely. The Boy was forced to take drastic measures and do the only thing he could... Downsize his organisation.

"Within weeks nearly two-hundred smugglers were put out of work. The town suffered badly whilst Jacob re-structured his entire organisation. Everybody knew The Boy was only doing what he had to, they didn't blame or even resent him, they knew who was causing the trouble... Rawlings and that he was protected by at least half a dozen soldiers at all times whilst he strolled through the town's cobbled streets. Jacob Swift knew he'd never be able to operate on the scale he had been, from then until the day he died he only worked alongside his set clan of men who'd earned his trust. Every one of them had played their part dealing with the Jenkins family and carried a secret that united them all together.

"Jacob still managed to successfully land cargoes but he switched tactics completely. He wasn't stupid either and knew he couldn't beat Rawlings so he let the magistrate have his victory and The Boy disappeared off the radar. He spent a long time lying low and keeping out of the public eye. Magistrate Rawlings canvassed the town for information leading to Jacob

Swift's whereabouts, but he had no luck. Nobody in the town knew.

"The Boy had vacated his town house and gone to ground. Jacob had more than a dozen safe houses where he stored cargo spread halfway across the county, only a handful of his men knew the locations and most of them had gone to ground alongside him. Jacob left a nurse to care for his father and Bates' old headquarters sat empty whilst Bill's will was executed.

"Hester kept Jacob's business afloat in his absence. The man with a head for figures worked selflessly for The Boy guaranteeing that a steady flow of goods hit the shores and an equally steady flow of profits were returned. Hester had been given strict instructions to help many of the local people in the town and during that period most of The Boys' profits were shared between the people who needed them. Even with everything that had happened Jacob Swift was still regarded as a hero around the town's cobbled streets and people missed him dearly.

"As the weeks passed to months The Boy slowly became a legend. Parents began telling tales of his adventures to their children before bed whilst Theodore Rawlings and his soldiers raided every tavern and drinking den in the area. They threatened and intimidated every drunk; snitch and crook in the town but nobody would give up Jacob's whereabouts.

"Bill had once taught Jacob the difference between fear and respect; local people were loyal to The Boy out of both. Jacob was going through tough times but they wouldn't last forever and nobody in the town was willing to make an enemy out of Jacob.

"Ronnie Jenkins had made that mistake and the huge man had been hacked to death with an axe for his troubles. So, for a while, Jacob lived in the shadows. He no longer mixed with the rich in the town's fancy restaurants. The Boy became a true outlaw, he was the king amongst smugglers and a legend in the town's shady underworld. Jacob Swift had shown the world what he was willing to sacrifice for one of his men and everybody loved him for it."

Chapter 32

"Over the next few months, Jacob Swift lived his life on the edge and risked his neck every day of the week; he had many close calls with the law and was nearly apprehended on several occasions. Magistrate Rawlings canvassed the town with wanted posters offering a handsome reward for any information leading to The Boy's arrest. Everyone in the town, young or old, rich or poor had seen the posters. They had a picture of Jacob's face on the front, a face everybody recognised. The sum of money Rawlings was offering was tempting for some, times were harder than ever but most of the town's locals were still loyal to their young friend.

"In the town, Jacob had employed hundreds and helped thousands over the years and the town hadn't forgotten. The wanted posters just added to Jacob's notoriety and, as time passed, he became a figure in the town's folklore, but it wasn't just The Boy who was wanted by the law either. The warrant for murder was still out on Jim Robson, Jacob's old school friend. The tubby boy who'd once been teased about his weight now had a reputation in the town equal to Alfie Bicks and was feared just as much.

"Occasionally, when Jacob was seen, usually in the dead of night with half a dozen of his most trusted bodyguards, tales would spread through the town's cobbled streets quicker than the wind that powered The Boy's clippers. On one particular night Jacob was seen making his way along the shore towards his old townhouse, it was really late but he was spotted by a local drunk named Kenny Lucas. Kenny had made his way up to the shore for some sea air after boozing in one of the town's taverns all night long. The drunk's desire for the reward on offer outweighed any loyalty he had for the town's youngest outlaw. Jacob wasn't alone that night, though, but when they reached his townhouse only The Boy and one of his bodyguards entered. That man was Thomas, Kenny was sure of that much and he wasted no time summoning the town's magistrate and spilling the beans.

"Theodore Rawlings was outraged when one of his servants woke him in the middle of the night, but, after hearing the news, he was out of bed and wide awake in moments with the prospect of finally catching Jacob Swift, the young man who'd made him a laughing stock amongst his superiors. Within the hour Jacob's townhouse was surrounded by soldiers from the local garrison and Theodore Rawlings was as smug as a Cheshire cat, confident that he'd finally caught Jacob Swift, the country's biggest smuggler.

"Soldiers armed with muskets and rifles covered the townhouse's exits and, as far as the magistrate could see, there was nowhere for young Jacob or his deadly bodyguard to escape. Rawlings gave the order to kill either man on site. Both had caused him too much trouble in the past.

"Meanwhile Jacob, unaware of the situation brewing outside, was talking to his father and drinking tea. Since becoming a wanted man he rarely got to spend time with his father and, when he did it was always under similar circumstances in the middle of the night. The pair was busy reminiscing about some of the characters they'd worked with on the fishing boats many years before. In an odd way Jacob's father was very proud of his son, he'd grown into a powerful and influential man, however the old fisherman often shed a tear for his only child whom he knew would inevitably be taken from him at some point or another.

"Thomas was in the front room watching the street outside in silence; suddenly the huge and emotionless bodyguard leapt to his feet and rushed through into the kitchen, startling both Jacob and his father. The pair stared up at Jacob's enforcer as his huge frame blocked the doorway. 'We got trouble, the house is surrounded', was all Thomas said, which was more than enough for his young boss to spring into action.

*

157

"Outside in the street Theodore Rawlings watched with a crooked smile on his face as one of his soldiers crept up to the townhouse. The soldier banged hard on the door with his fist and within moments, to everybody's surprise it swung open.

"Rawlings could feel his heart beating inside his chest. 'Maybe Jacob was about to surrender?' he wondered. Rawlings was going to kill him anyway. The magistrate had no choice he'd been taking bribes off The Boy for a long time before the pair had fallen out and Jacob knew way too much, enough to put Rawlings behind bars forever. But, much to Rawlings' disappointment, it was Jacob's father who stepped out of the townhouse with his hands held high and a look of despair on his face. Immediately he was dragged aside as half a dozen soldiers poured into the house.

"Several very slow and anxious minutes passed by for Magistrate Rawlings who was beginning to get a bad feeling deep down in his guts, it was a feeling he recognised. He'd got it in the market square on the morning of Jim Robson's execution as he'd clapped eyes on Jacob trotting through the crowds on his white horse as bold as brass. The magistrate began to fear that even more humiliation was on its way.

"A moment later one of his soldiers exited the house and marched over to where Rawlings was stood. 'We've searched the entire house, it's empty sir,' he reported as the magistrate stood in shock whilst the news sunk in and blood rushed to his face, then he cursed loudly and stamped his feet in anger before searching the crowd for the drunkard Kenny Lucas, the man who was responsible for yet another blunder.

"Finally the pair caught eye contact and Rawlings marched up to him red-faced, Kenny Lucas cowered as the magistrate shouted in his face. 'You told me he went inside,' the magistrate roared.

"'He did, I promise governor, I saw it with my own eyes I did,' Kenny pleaded.

"'Yeah after drinking your own weight in rum,' Rawlings spat out before turning to his soldiers. 'Lock this man up for wasting my time,' he ordered.

"Kenny Lucas was seized by several of the soldiers who

began shackling him, he pleaded with the magistrate but Rawlings was no longer listening, as far as he was concerned the drunk had wasted enough of his time and he shouldn't have listened to him in the first place. He ordered the troops back to the barracks and retired home to bed once more, he was angry at having his time wasted but Rawlings had no idea just how close he'd come that night to catching Jacob Swift and his most ruthless bodyguard.

"Over the previous months the magistrate had been busy in his quest to catch Jacob, but Jacob and his gang had been very busy too. Being a wanted man made travelling from place to place very risky for Jacob; everybody in the town knew his face and it was inevitable that somebody would eventually give into the temptation and take a big dirty bite at the hook being offered as a reward for his capture.

"In the week following Jim Robson's escape from the noose, whilst hiding out on a farm out of town, young Jacob had experienced a moment of clarity. Not for the first time in his life, The Boy had been struck with an idea and he'd wasted no time putting it into action. Jacob struggled moving around the town unseen, the labyrinth of crisscrossing cobbled streets were usually busy and often enough soldiers were posted as lookouts. The Boy realised that he needed another way of travelling, a way that guaranteed he could move unseen. The idea struck him one day when he was talking to Alfie and the tall bodyguard was telling him about a part of the chalk cliffs up near Bates' old headquarters that had collapsed onto the beach, this happened from time to time, the ground in the whole area was made of chalk and it was as soft as cheese.

"Jacob had lapsed into silence lost in his own thoughts when Alfie turned to him.

"'You alright Boss?' he asked. Jacob was more than alright he'd just realised something that would prove invaluable in the years to come. He realised that day how easy it would be to build a secret tunnel network from one place to another, the town's cobbled streets were like a labyrinth and everybody had a cellar.

So Jacob had set a team to work immediately and for six

solid weeks a dozen of his strongest men worked tirelessly creating a network of secret tunnels and escapes from place to place hidden under the town's cobbled streets. That night at his townhouse was the first of many occasions when Jacob found it necessary to use them.

"In the years to come he'd find them invaluable as not just a method of escape, but as a route to transport and store his smuggled merchandise. Eventually, the network would link up to dozens of houses owned by his men, to taverns that would sell his smuggled liquor and, of course, to countless escape hatches like the one Thomas and Jacob had used on that first night.

"Many were hidden right up on the shoreline where boats could pull up on the shingle and stow their cargoes out of sight. In order to survive, Jacob used his wits and learnt many new tactics, being hunted just made him smarter and stronger and, as time passed, The Boy and his gang's confidence grew."

Chapter 33

"It was on a cold winter night whilst Jacob was struggling to navigate one of his cutters on a rough and dangerous sea when luck finally shone down on The Boy. Jacob had visited France to meet one of the merchants he traded with. The trip had gone well up until half way home. Jacob had estimated his cutter was only ten miles off the English coast when a storm appeared from nowhere. The Channel was blown by mighty gusts of wind in every direction. Huge white horses appeared on the crests of waves that crashed relentlessly down on Jacob's small ship.

"The Boys' crew held on for dear life. Like Jacob himself, they were the best of the best, tough men that lived and breathed for the wind on their backs and salt air in their lungs. Over the years they'd all experienced everything the ocean could throw at them and lived to tell the tales, that day they were making progress across The Channel confident they could use the harsh conditions to their advantage and reach home shores without any encounters with the Customs and Excise men.

"Jacob's ship, like always on a return journey from the continent, was loaded to the hilt with a selection of smuggled goods. The cutter had sailed at least four miles through one of the harshest seas Jacob had ever experienced when The Boy first saw it. At first it was just a speck on the horizon, a black dot that disappeared and reappeared every time the cutter reached the crest of another wave. Whilst they were blown closer and closer Jacob's curiosity grew and grew.

"Eventually he pulled out his telescope, peering through he immediately made out a ship in distress; it had been blown over and was being smashed to pieces by the brutal sea. Jacob knew at least a dozen men who would be out salvaging the vessel and whatever cargo she carried as soon as the storm died down. This wasn't Jacob's line of work though. He was a smuggler through and through. Salvaging he left to the town's longshoremen. But then The Boy caught a glimpse of something in the water that grabbed his attention immediately.

"Clinging onto the hull of the upturned vessel and fighting for his life was a lone figure, a crew member of the disaster stricken vessel struggling for survival against an ocean that had no forgiveness and no mercy. Jacob Swift turned to face his ship's captain who was out on deck clinging on for dear life as waves crashed around him.

"'Alter your course,' Jacob shouted over the roar of the ocean. 'Take us close to that vessel,' he ordered.

"The captain nodded and got straight to work, a moment later the cutter swung around and crested a huge wave. Jacob watched with curiosity as the disaster-stricken vessel got closer and closer. The ship's crew member was alive, just about, but Jacob could see that if he spent any longer in the water The Channel would claim yet another life. He clung onto the upturned vessel exhausted as waves broke around him threatening to pull him under into the salty depths. Jacob Swift couldn't leave a fellow sailor in distress even though he knew he would be taking a great risk offering assistance, he knew plenty of other smugglers who would have turned the other cheek.

"Jacob took a few deep breaths and shouted more orders across the deck, orders that were nearly lost in the howling wind, but his captain nodded with respect for his young boss who was willing to risk everything for a complete stranger. A moment later, he altered the ship's course yet again whilst Jacob fastened a rope around his waist. Most men would have shaken in their boots at the thought of jumping overboard into a sea as rough but Jacob Swift had been living in fear and watching over his shoulder for so long that he'd become almost conditioned to danger.

"The Boy took one big deep breath and prepared himself for the cold as his smuggling ship approached the upturned vessel, and then he dived overboard into the rough and freezing water. Immediately he was dragged under and smashed around, when he finally surfaced he struggled to get his bearings as waves crashed over him. A moment later he was dragged under once more. He kicked and kicked until he surfaced again. Then in the nick of time he'd spotted the hull of the upturned ship, it was disappearing and reappearing as waves crashed over her.

"Jacob swam with all his might making slow progress. When he did reach her he clung on for dear life much like its sole survivor. Adrenaline raced through his veins as he caught his breath and got his bearings. Jacob searched frantically until he spotted the man clinging onto the rudder of the upturned vessel, then summoning all his strength he swam towards him.

"The man had spotted Jacob and was staring in shock at what he was witnessing, through glassy eyes he watched as Jacob approached him getting smashed by waves from every angle. Finally Jacob reached the man who was pale and shaking badly; he'd clearly been in the water for a great deal of time.

"'It's alright my friend,' Jacob shouted above the roar of the ocean the pair were smashed by another wave which nearly pulled them both under the murky depths, but then relief flooded through young Jacob as he felt the pull of rope around his waist as his cutter's crew began the laborious task of pulling their young leader back to safety.

"A short time later Jacob was back aboard his own ship, in a small cabin below deck trying to warm his bones. The Boy had only been in the water for a short time but it had been long enough. The stranger sat a few feet in front of him wrapped in blankets; he hadn't said a word since he'd boarded Jacob's vessel. Jacob could see the man was in shock. He'd been close to death and was still coming to terms with it. His eyes roamed the small cabin, always falling on Jacob whom he would stare at briefly before beginning the cycle once again. A few of Jacob's crew stood around watching the stranger suspiciously ready to pounce and pin the man to the decks if he made a single move towards their leader, who'd risked way too much for their liking as it was.

"It was Jacob himself who broke the silence, turning to one

of his men he ordered two glasses of brandy, a commodity that wasn't exactly in short supply aboard The Boy's ship which was loaded to the hilt with it. Jacob rarely drank and preferred to have a clear mind at all times but he'd frozen half to death and needed a nip to warm himself up. Both men were handed a brandy, the stranger held the glass in front of him, Jacob noted some blood had returned to his face and he was looking better as the minutes passed.

"The man was looking around the cabin at the dozens of casks of spirits and bales of tobacco until Jacob raised his glass which caught the man's attention.

"'To your life, my brother,' Jacob toasted whilst the man stared at him for a moment with a crooked smile on his face.

"'And to yours, my young friend, the bravest man I've ever met,' he said before they both gulped their drinks. Then Jacob reached out and extended his hand and the man gripped it tightly, instantly one of Jacob's men stepped forward and pulled out a musket but The Boy waved him away and stared hard at the stranger.

"'I'm Jacob…' he attempted to say but the man cut in.

"'Swift,' he finished in a well-spoken voice. 'The Boy, the king of smugglers so they say. You were raised by a fisherman on these very waters and know them better than anybody. Taken in by a man named Billy Bates and trained from a very young age to land cargoes on these shores with an efficiency unmatched by anyone in this country.' Silence settled over the small cabin, the only noises being the creaking of the vessel as it mounted waves and the howling wind.

"Jacob was staring into the man's eyes, curious to know why this stranger knew so much about him. His men were on edge now. The stranger had justified their suspicions.

"'And you are?' Jacob finally asked.

"The stranger smiled. 'Up until an hour ago, I was an enemy of yours, but now you must consider me a friend. You took a great risk helping me. You're an exceptionally brave young man you could have easily perished alongside my crew.'

Jacob nodded. 'How many?' he asked the stranger who

looked down at the floor before looking into The Boy's eyes. 'Four, good men too,' he replied with emotion in his voice.

'I'm sorry to hear that, this Channel is unforgiving,' Jacob stated as the stranger nodded and smiled.

'I owe you a great debt, Mr. Swift, and I swear on the blood of my family I will pay you back. My full title is Admiral Philip Saunders, Captain of the H.M.S Windsor. My ship has been dispatched by King George to patrol these waters and from this day forth my friend I grant you safe passage,' The stranger said, receiving gasps of surprise from most of the men present. The Boy stared in shock at the man in front of him; he knew his ships. Bill had taught him all about the naval fleet.

"'The Windsor's a man-of-war, a seventy gunner,' Jacob said, still astonished by the situation he'd found himself in.

"'That she is, my boy. She's one of the greatest ships this world has ever seen and she's at your disposal,' the Admiral replied.

"Jacob Swift rubbed his chin and thought about how useful an ally in the Royal Navy could prove to be, things were finally turning around for The Boy."

Chapter 34

"Several days after Jacob's chance encounter out in The Channel, the Admiral sent a messenger into the town's dangerous cobbled streets. Through a network of local men who were loyal to The Boy and his small band of outlaws word reached Jacob Swift's ears. Admiral Philip Saunders wanted a meeting with Jacob, a meeting that roused The Boy's suspicions from the very start. He was always on the lookout for a trap. Having a price on his head, he had to be on the ball twenty-four hours a day. Jacob had saved the Admiral's life but the man was still a naval officer and an employee of the Crown, to which Jacob was costing a fortune in lost revenue.

"In the end The Boy agreed to attend the meeting, but only if it was held within his territory at a location of his choice where he knew he'd be safe. Jacob brought a dozen of his men who were all carrying firearms with them just in case the Admiral tried to bring England's most notorious smuggler to justice, a feat that Jacob had no doubt would bring huge recognition to the Admiral. Among Jacob's men were Jim Robson, Thomas and Alfie Bicks who was now fully recovered from the savage beating Big Ronnie and his clan had given him, he bore a few scars but Jacob's tall bodyguard had been very lucky.

"The meeting was held in a tavern close to Prosperity Farm, and, when Jacob arrived, the Admiral was already seated at a table in the corner with a few of his men, but he quickly rose to his feet and greeted The Boy warmly before they all sat down and began negotiations. Saunders was good to his word and eager to repay the debt he owed Jacob for saving his skin, and much to The Boy and his gang's complete surprise the Admiral offered them all a deal. He wanted Jacob and his men to enlist in the Royal Navy and work under his command, assuring them they'd all receive a full pardon for their smuggling crimes.

"'Mr. Swift, we need men like you with knowledge of the sea, experience and above all courage. You could go all the way. I know you're loyal to your men,' the Admiral said looking over at Jacob's bodyguards who were all glaring back at him. 'But I'm offering you all a lifeline. I've taken the time to look into your situation and it has to be said you've made a fair few enemies in your short years. If you join me then all of your troubles can be swept under the carpet. It could be like a fresh start for all of you,' he promised.

"The room fell silent as Jacob thought hard about the offer. He didn't doubt the man in front of him. Billy Bates had taught Jacob how to tell when somebody was deceiving him and Philip Saunders was genuine. He was an Admiral in the Royal Fleet and surely had enough pull in the government, Jacob had heard of dozens of fellow smugglers who'd made the leap to the Navy in the past. But Jacob Swift was a smuggler through and through and his men; men like Thomas depended on him. They'd never take orders from others. Jacob would have been happy out on the open sea by Philip Saunders' side but he politely declined in the end because of a promise he'd made to Billy Bates several years before.

"Admiral Saunders rubbed his chin and smiled giving young Jacob the distinct impression he'd received the answer he'd expected, after a long moment he looked into The Boy's eyes. 'If you ever change your mind, the offer's always open. You're a very smart and brave young man and it would be a pleasure to work alongside you, but, in the meantime Mr. Swift, I hope you can let me pay the debt I owe to you and your men for saving my life,' the Admiral said, and now it was time for a smile to creep up on young Jacob's face.

"That day The Boy made a deal with Admiral Saunders, a deal that not only repaid the debt Jacob Swift was owed but was also financially rewarding to the Admiral and his men. From that day forth Jacob was able to rely on the H.M.S Windsor, a virtually unsinkable seventy gun man-of-war to transport a steady flow of his smuggled goods across the English Channel. Jacob still used his fleet of cutters to bring merchandise into the country providing him with far more merchandise on his hands to transport and sell, and as a result far more profits.

"The Boy set his man Hester, the mathematician, to work and for the first time in a long while Jacob Swift had goods flowing across the county once again. Within weeks, The Boy had access to a greater flow of cash, he paid the Admiral generously to keep his men happy and in return the Admiral fed Jacob with information from the highest level, information that proved priceless to Jacob.

"The Boy and his gang were still wanted by the crooked Magistrate Theodore Rawlings, Customs and Excise men as well as soldiers of the Crown. On land in the town's cobbled and dangerous streets they were hunted like dogs but in The Channel where it mattered it was a different story. Jacob Swift could relax knowing that he could travel to and from the continent in relative safety. Thanks to the Admiral he was well aware of any naval ships in the area several days in advance.

"With a greater flow of smuggled goods hitting the markets, word soon spread through the town's cobbled streets and into villages across the county. The Boy had finally stepped out of the shadows. Magistrate Rawlings had won the battle driving Jacob and his gang underground, but there was no doubt in anybody's mind who'd won the war.

"Local people began describing the town's young friend as untouchable. He'd saved them from the savage Jenkins clan and laughed in the face of the law. Jacob Swift was one of their own and people loved him for it."

Chapter 35

"For the first time in a very long time Jacob Swift ventured out during the day into the town's cobbled streets and life as he knew it changed in the blink of an eye. He knew that he was taking a risk that day, the streets were bustling with people travelling to and fro from the town's market and the magistrate was bound to be about looking for trouble, but Jacob had spent a long time in hiding, moving around underground through his own labyrinth of tunnels he'd simply had enough. Danger had become such a large part of The Boy's life that he'd become accustomed to it. On that day when Jacob had strolled through the towns cobbled streets every person stopped and stared in shock, many bowed and tried to approach him to offer their thanks for the good deeds he'd done for them in the past.

"In short, The Boy caught everyone's attention but none more than Elizabeth Swan who could only smile shyly in Jacob's direction. Elizabeth was the younger sister of Michael Swan, a local smuggler who had worked alongside The Boy for years. Michael was as loyal as the day was long, he'd been one of the first people Jacob had employed back in the day when Billy Bates had run the town and had been in the woods on that dreaded morning when the Jenkins clan had met their bloody end. Michael had been true to his word, he had never spoken about what had taken place, not even to his younger sister. Elizabeth had seen Jacob Swift on several occasions and knew exactly who he was. She was only seventeen years old with brown eyes and curly brown hair that fell to her shoulders, and pretty even in the rags that she wore.

Disappointingly for Elizabeth as Jacob strolled towards where she was stood admiring him, he failed to notice her or so she thought. In truth Jacob had, but the young man who led the biggest smuggling organisation the country had ever seen was surprisingly timid and shy around women. Jacob noticed her staring his way out of the corner of his eye, but he was suddenly distracted by the sounds of heels on the cobbled street and swung around to face a sight that sent shivers down his spine. Running towards him at the end of the street were a dozen soldiers armed with rifles and, much to Jacob's surprise, it was Rawlings himself leading the charge. The corrupt and bulbous magistrate was running with all his might with a look of satisfaction on his chubby face. It took only a split second for Jacob Swift's world to erupt into chaos. Most of the locals who only moments earlier had been praising him dropped him like a lead weight and ran for safety. The Boy cursed himself for not bringing his most trusted bodyguards with him into the town, the handful he had were inexperienced and panicked as soon as Rawlings gave chase.

"Jacob Swift stood for a moment like a rabbit in the headlights watching as Rawlings and his men edged closer and closer. The Boy watched as his life flashed before his eyes and for a moment that lasted a lifetime Jacob was helpless, and in that moment an angel came to his rescue. Suddenly a hand grabbed him and pulled him through into an alleyway off the street... that hand belonged to Elizabeth Swan. The pair ran through a network of alleys with Rawlings and his men giving chase every step of the way. Jacob would have been captured and hanged that day if it hadn't been for Elizabeth who led the young smuggler down into an old cellar that was boarded up with wooden slats.

"The pair waited for the magistrate and his soldiers to pass, pressed tightly against each other virtually in the dark with the only light coming from the cracks between the slats above them at street level. For a long moment they stared into each other's eyes, both short of breath and struggling to breathe quietly. Elizabeth Swan smiled, like everyone in the town who'd grown up without two pennies to rub together, she had spent her childhood hearing stories about Jacob Swift... the most successful smuggler in the country. Stories that had spread across the land and would eventually lead to his downfall.

"But on that day Elizabeth knew she'd never get another

opportunity to get this close to Jacob Swift who was usually flanked by bodyguards at all times. Jacob was staring at Elizabeth, lost in her beauty. He noticed her smile and returned it before both of them struggled not to laugh and give away their location.

"It was Elizabeth, the shy young girl, who decided not to waste the opportunity that fate had presented her. She leant forward and kissed Jacob, who up until that day had always had complete control of his emotions, but in that moment he experienced an emotion he'd never felt before and Jacob, a young man who people looked up to, had no idea how to deal with it. He felt like he'd been hit with a 20lb cannonball straight in the chest and Jacob wasn't alone either.

"The pair fell in love immediately and from that day forth they were inseparable. They both came from similar backgrounds, both had been raised in poverty and both had survived on what scraps the sea had offered."

Chapter 36

"The beginning of the end for Jacob Swift as England's youngest, most notorious and successful smuggler began neither in the town's cobbled streets, nor out on The Channel where he'd been raised but thousands of miles away in a far, far off land. The Boy's career became unknowingly caught up in a chain of events that were destined to lead to his downfall. Ironically it was all because of his good nature and willingness to help others, others that were way beyond help. In the end young Jacob became the target of a man far more dangerous and powerful than anybody he'd ever done business with in all his years on this earth. A well-spoken, educated man who wouldn't dare tread the town's cobbled streets alone, but was much more dangerous than a hundred men like Thomas.

"A long time before Jacob Swift had even been born, a trading company had been established in India with the sole intention of bringing spices back to England. It was named the East India Trading Company and it slowly prospered; within a hundred years it had trading posts all over India. The company thrived for a long time on the spice trade earning good money, and, as time passed, others were tempted by the riches India had to offer and the French soon arrived. Then the inevitable happened, war broke out and soldiers of the Crown slaughtered many poor Indian people caught up in the crossfire.

"The British Army rolled through India's country and culture destroying everything it touched. Villages were burned to the ground whilst temples were ransacked and destroyed by people whose greed far outweighed their sense of right and wrong. Dozens of Hindu temples were pillaged. For thousands of years the Indian people had worshipped sacred jewels. Diamonds, rubies and emeralds as large as golf balls were considered to be gifts from the heavens and the tears of the gods.

"Originally, most of the largest precious stones in the world belonged to India; they were found under the fields and in the rivers, worshipped by a race of peaceful people who had strong beliefs in their powers. The Hindu people believed the gems helped their country prosper and kept their land fertile. During those years of unrest, many Hindu relics were stolen from temples across the land, treasures that found their way onto merchant ships and sailed away from India never to return. One of these relics was a red ruby. They say it was the size of a man's fist, if the stories are to be believed. The ruby was the largest the world had ever seen. It had been worshipped in India for centuries.

"The man who stole the ruby in the first place was a British politician named Cecil Blackheath. In the early 1790's he'd been sent out to India to oversee the British Army's operations and report back to parliament. But Cecil was a greedy and corrupt man and, as soon as he landed on Indian soil and witnessed first-hand the riches that were on offer, his priorities changed somewhat. Cecil Blackheath decided that he would use his trip overseas to set him up financially for life. He planned on gathering a little hoard of treasure for his retirement. It was all too much of a temptation for Blackheath who had hundreds of troops at his disposal, men that would do his dirty work without even realising it.

"It was a simple plan. The country was in chaos; Cecil figured that he could order his troops to ransack the temple at Mysore where the jewel was kept and steal it. Cecil planned on bringing it back to Blighty on one of the East India Company's ships. He was good friends with a corrupt merchant whose greed matched his own. Cecil promised to make the man richer than his wildest dreams. Maybe Cecil Blackheath carried out his promise, we'll never know for sure. The politician had a contact in the city that could sell the stone, a jeweller who knew many rich men with private collections equal to the Crown Jewels. Cecil planned on stashing up a fortune for his later years in life but the politician had overlooked one thing… destiny.

"According to the story the merchant smuggled the ruby

back on the trading ship; they sailed for weeks and weeks until they finally reached British waters where they eventually dropped anchor in the downs just off our coast. Then the unimaginable happened, the merchant ship was attacked in the night by a small gang of thieves... and the ruby was stolen from the merchant who'd helped steal it in the first place.

Chapter 37

"On the 27th September 1792 Jacob Swift married the only woman he'd ever loved, Elizabeth Swan. It was a joyous occasion, a day The Boy would hold close to his heart until the day he died, but, unknown to young Jacob that day wasn't far off. Jacob's wedding day was like the calm before the storm, but this storm wasn't going to blow over for The Boy who was still only twenty-two years old.

"The wedding ceremony was held in a small chapel overlooking the English Channel, a place that was close to both their hearts. On that special day the chapel was packed with all the usual faces. The Boy stood at the front nervous for once in his life. Jim Robson stood at his side as best man. In the front row stood Jacob's father, the man had tears in his eyes way before the service had even begun. To his left side stood Thomas, Jacob's most feared bodyguard, who had a smile on his face but showed none of the same emotions as the man standing next to him. Alfie Bicks was there too, looking proudly at The Boy he'd watched grow into a man. Further back in the crowd stood Hester, the mathematician, and Havelock, the farmer. Even Admiral Philip Saunders had turned up to watch the notorious smuggler who'd saved his skin tie the knot. The wedding had been organized with security in mind. Jacob wanted to enjoy the day knowing that no uninvited guests were going to show their faces, especially the puffy-round face of Magistrate Rawlings, the man who wanted revenge on Jacob more than anyone. It was no secret in the cobbled streets that the town's 'young friend' was going to marry. As a precaution the location of the ceremony was kept a closely guarded secret, even the guests didn't know. Jacob dispatched fifty of his most trusted men to pick them up and bring them to the ceremony. Those men stood outside guarding the chapel from every angle with bats at their sides and muskets hidden in their jackets.

"When Elizabeth Swan entered the chapel there was a gasp from the crowd of misfits and vagrants gathered inside. To Jacob she looked more beautiful than anything he'd ever seen. She wore a white lace dress he'd brought over from Paris on board one of his many ships. Elizabeth's older brother Michael, a close friend of Jacob's, walked her up the aisle. Then the young lovers stared into each other's eyes and gave their wedding vows, binding themselves to each other in the eyes of God.

"After the ceremony, the reception was held up on the cliffs near Billy Bates' old headquarters. The house overlooking The Channel was now legally Thomas's. The old man with the eyes like black marbles had given Jacob Swift his empire in life, but in death Bill had handed all of his worldly possessions to the orphan he'd taken in from the streets and raised as a son.

"All afternoon a band played tunes that whistled out from the cliff tops and over The Channel whilst people danced and drank an endless supply of smuggled liquor. Many of Jacob's gang gave speeches, congratulating the happy couple and publicly thanking Jacob for all he'd done for them over the years.

"Elizabeth was presented with so many gifts that day she was overwhelmed. She'd grown up with nothing and deep down the only thing she needed was the young man at her side, but she thanked everyone for their generosity. Of all the gifts she received that day, the biggest surprise was from an old boat builder who'd carved a figurehead of her out of oak; it was to be attached to the stern of one of Jacob's ships. It wasn't completely finished but the old carpenter told Jacob it was so that she'd always be near him, even when he was out on The Channel."

*

"Oh my God!" young Stanley said out loud interrupting Reg Cooper's story, but the museum's old curator didn't mind.

He sat there with a big grin on his face as he watched young Stan race over to the figurehead in the corner of the museum through his thick spectacles. Stan stared up at the carving of Elizabeth in amazement before he turned to Reg. "So how did you get your hands on it?" he asked Reg who pushed his glasses back up the bridge of his nose and chuckled to himself.

"Well I suppose that's part of the story, come take a seat and you'll find out," he replied, a moment later Stan was seated next to him waiting for him to continue.

*

"At one stage during that day's festivities, Jacob noticed Thomas stood away from the crowd staring out at The Channel and the ships passing to and fro in the distance. The Boy approached him slowly until he was stood at his side; Thomas glanced to his left and smiled before putting one of his huge arms round Jacob and pulling his boss close.

"'You know, Jacob, you're the closest thing I've got to family now,' the fearless bodyguard said as they both stared at the horizon. 'If anything ever happened to you I'd have no-one.' Jacob thought for a moment. He knew that in the weeks following Bill's death he'd become closer in a way to Thomas than he'd ever been with Alfie or even Jim.

"'Brother, I'm not going anywhere, we'll always be at each other's side,' he said from deep down in his heart. Thomas nodded before he ruffled Jacob's blond hair then the pair raised a toast to Billy Bates, the man that had brought them together, the man they both missed dearly.

*

"Later that evening when the sun had fallen out of the sky Theodore Rawlings staggered out of the inn where he'd been boozing, it was dark and for once he had none of his men at his side. He buttoned up his coat before glancing either way up the cobbled street. A mist had drifted in off The Channel bringing visibility down to less than a dozen yards. Rawlings felt quite

177

vulnerable and had a bad feeling deep down in his guts. He wasted no time and began marching in the direction of his house. Appearing through the mist in front of him Rawlings could make out the light of a lantern getting brighter and brighter.

"Suddenly Rawlings faced a sight that made him stop-dead in his tracks. Thomas, The Boy's most ruthless bodyguard appeared from nowhere blocking his path. The huge man held up his lantern illuminating his emotionless face. Theodore Rawlings was frozen to the spot terrified. He'd expected Jacob Swift to send one of his men to kill him for a long time; Rawlings feared that moment had finally arrived. The magistrate had known Jacob's ruthless bodyguard since the days when he'd lived on the streets robbing sailors to survive, he knew what the huge man was capable of. Rawlings had no evidence but he knew deep down that it had been the man in front of him who had hacked Big Ronnie Jenkins to death.

"Thomas leant in towards Rawlings until their noses were only inches apart, the magistrate swallowed hard as he stared into Thomas's vacant eyes. 'I bring a message to you from Jacob Swift, he says that if you or any of your men ever go within a dozen feet of Elizabeth Swan you'll all die painful deaths, you understand?' Thomas demanded as Rawlings nodded petrified.

"'Remember that you only breathe because The Boy lets you. He can have you executed anytime he wants, just like that,' Thomas warned before blowing out the flame of his lantern and vanishing into the shadows.

"Theodore Rawlings stood alone in the dark once more, breathing deeply and trying to get himself together. Jacob Swift rarely sent messages, the magistrate knew that he needed to heed Thomas's stark warning and leave Elizabeth Swan well alone or pay the consequences with his life, and Rawlings knew that Jacob's men would take it from him very slowly for old time's sake. The magistrate hated Jacob Swift with a passion, The Boy had made him look like a fool on countless occasions. Whilst Rawlings marched home through the mist that night he prayed that Jacob would one day come unstuck and finally receive the punishment he deserved. Rawlings dreamt of that day knowing he'd watch with a smile on his face. But Rawlings didn't know that it was destined to be that very night when things began to go wrong for the town's young friend and most notorious smuggler.

*

"Several hours later in the dead of the night when the town's lights had finally gone out four desperate thieves carried their rowing galley down the shingle beach and into the calm water of the English Channel. The mist that had drifted in off the sea hours earlier had cleared and a full moon lit up the sky as the thieves rowed out in silence towards a merchant ship on the horizon that they planned to rob; the only noise came from the waves lapping at the shore and their oars cutting into the water. The four thieves were locals, born and bred in the town's cobbled streets. They'd never before tried to steal from one of the East India's merchant ships but times were harder than ever and they had little choice.

"When they finally reached the ship, the gang's leader Eddie Biggs scanned the deck for any night watchmen making their rounds before giving his men the nod to climb aboard. The men pulled masks over their faces and were armed with clubs and a single musket when they climbed up onto the deck of the huge ship, a ship that had sailed half way around the world and back to bring the treasures it had stowed onboard.

"Feeling more scared than he'd ever been in his life, Eddie led his gang in silence to the captain's cabin where they slipped inside and woke the man with the musket pressed to his face. He stared in shock for a moment still half asleep before he finally mumbled, 'You'll never get away with this,' through gritted teeth. A moment later the thieves gagged him and tied him up. They knew that it would only take a single scream from the Captain to wake the rest of the ship, and then the thieves wouldn't have stood a chance. The hardened sailors aboard that were tucked up in their cabins would tear them apart before throwing their remains overboard.

"Eddie searched the captain's cabin for the safe, the ship was on its return journey but Eddie knew it would still hold some cash. He finally found it tucked away in the corner of the cabin. Threatening the Captain with the musket once more Eddie demanded the safe's key, which he found tied to a piece of string around the man's neck. The Captain could see that Eddie and his men were desperate. The Captain had no choice but to hand it over. Eddie Biggs wasted no time clearing the small safe out and throwing its contents into a sack, he wanted off the ship as soon as possible.

"The thieves left the Captain gagged knowing that he'd be found in the morning. Whilst Eddie and his men rowed back over the calm sea towards the town they were all overwhelmed by the success of the raid. But, unknown to the thieves, they'd just signed their own death warrants and that of many others. Hidden in a small box at the bottom of the sack was a precious stone that didn't belong to the East India Trading Company. It belonged to a very dangerous politician named Cecil Blackheath, a man who would stop at nothing to get it back and kill everyone in his path. The stone was a red ruby the size of a man's fist and had been named because its colour matched the eyes of a rather deadly snake native to India, a ruby that had been stolen only months earlier from a Hindu temple a lifetime away, a ruby known in India as the Eye of the Serpent."

Chapter 38

"The what?" Stanley found himself blurting out, echoing through the still empty museum. Reg glanced his way, startled, as Stanley's heart began to beat deep inside his chest, unknown to him his jaw had dropped and he was sat staring at old Reg, the museum's curator in amazement. For a long moment, Reg Cooper paused from recounting the story he'd spent a lifetime researching and stared at young Stanley, the boy who'd strolled into his museum and life the day before asking questions about a man that Reg had spent years trying to forget about.

"Are you ok lad? You've gone a funny colour," the old man asked as he pushed the spectacles back up the bridge of his nose.

But young Stanley was much more than just ok, his imagination was running away with him. Unknown to Reg, Stan had heard of the Eye of the Serpent before in Jacob's message that he'd found on the beach, the message that had brought him to the small museum in the first place.

The young boy turned to Reg the old museum's curator. "You said that some people don't believe in the story. What did you mean?" he demanded.

Reg Cooper stared in shock at Stan's sudden eagerness, he pondered for a moment before replying. "Some people believe that Jacob Swift never had the stone and that The Boy was used as a scapegoat, just somebody the real thief pinned the blame on. Jacob had certainly made enough enemies," Reg said.

"What it didn't exist?" Stan asked, Reg smiled.

"Oh it existed all right, back in India hundreds of years ago in the past, but then it was stolen and it disappeared forever."

Stanley was speechless. All of his hopes and dreams had been crushed. Only a moment earlier he'd been fantasizing about a treasure that was priceless. A treasure that would change his life forever and take him and his mum out of the shoebox flat they lived in. Stanley felt utterly deflated but then a seed of hope appeared and he jumped out of his seat. Jacob had the Eye of the Serpent. The Boy mentioned it in the message. The ruby *had* fallen into Jacob's hands.

For a moment Stan stood gathering his thoughts, a moment later he turned to old Reg who was staring at him with a look of concern on his face. Stanley debated about telling the museum's curator about the message and decided the time had finally come. He turned to Reg and just as he was about to open his mouth the old man beat him to it and began narrating the story once again.

Chapter 39

"The day after his wedding Jacob Swift and his wife left the town's cobbled streets and made their way to a small cottage on the outskirts of Kent that was set in the middle of acres of woodland overlooking a beautiful lake. The young couple spent an entire week wrapped in each other's arms planning their future. They played around swimming in the lake, picking wildflowers and chopping wood for the roaring fire they gathered around every evening. Thomas and a handful of his most trusted men went with them for protection, but Thomas and his men kept out of the newlyweds' way.

*

"Meanwhile the merchant ship belonging to the East India Trading Company had raised its mighty anchor and sailed from the Kent coast into the estuary of the River Thames where it eventually docked in Deptford. The ship's captain feeling very frightened and humiliated climbed onto dry land and boarded a horse and cart, destined for the Houses of Parliament and a meeting with Cecil Blackheath. The merchant was terrified about Blackheath's reaction when he heard about the theft; the crooked politician was as ruthless as they came. An hour later the merchant was seated in Blackheath's office sipping brandy to settle his nerves and pouring his heart out to the politician, whose expression of shock rapidly turned to anger on hearing of the theft of his most prized possession. Blackheath was devastated by the news; he'd spent months in a country he detested planning the raid on the temple to get his greedy hands on the jewel in the first place. Then he'd suffered for months waiting for the merchant ship to bring his stone to England's shores. Months that he'd spent dreaming of his retirement and planning what he was going to do with his newfound wealth. Now somebody had dared to steal those dreams and boy was Blackheath going to make them pay. In a fit of rage the politician grabbed the nearest thing at hand, a glass inkwell on his desk and launched it at a wall where it landed with a crash and shattered into a thousand pieces.

"The merchant in front of him cowered and stared at the floor terrified whilst Blackheath took a deep breath in an attempt to calm down. Then Blackheath interrogated the merchant for descriptions of the thieves, noting down exactly what the men had looked like before dismissing the merchant. Cecil Blackheath needed to be alone to gather his thoughts and form his plan of attack. The stone belonged to him, he'd stolen it once thousands of miles away in a far-off land and he'd steal it again. Blackheath figured that the robbery hadn't been planned, nobody knew about the priceless stone so the thieves were local bandits who'd stumbled upon it by pure luck. Cecil knew more than anyone how rare the ruby was and knew the thieves would face a near impossible task selling the stone without bringing serious attention down on themselves. Feeling a surge of re-assurance, Blackheath gritted his teeth and glanced at a map on the wall next to a deep black smear where the inkwell had exploded earlier. The politician's eyes traced the coastline of Kent until they settled on the spot where the merchant ship had been attacked; it was just off the coast of Deal, a town notorious for its smuggling.

"Immediately one name sprang to Blackheath's mind and that name was Jacob Swift. Cecil had heard all about the king of smugglers or The Boy as he was known, he'd been a topic of conversation at several dinner parties Blackheath had attended not to mention in the Houses of Parliament. Smuggling and how to deal with it had been a hot topic for years amongst politicians. The trade was costing the government a fortune in lost revenue and nowhere more so than on that notorious stretch of Kent's coast. Whilst pouring himself a large brandy Blackheath thought hard about the whole situation. The crooked politician concluded that, if The Boy hadn't orchestrated the robbery which Blackheath doubted, Jacob was far too smart to attack an East India ship, then he would certainly know who had. If the rumours were true about The Boy, then nothing happened near that town without his knowledge or even approval in most cases. Sipping his brandy Blackheath smiled whilst a plan formulated in his mind. In the end it was simple; Jacob was the key to getting the stone back. Blackheath was going to tear Jacob Swift's smuggling empire to shreds unless The Boy would cut a deal and return the ruby back to its rightful owner, and by that Blackheath meant himself.

"The politician chuckled as he thought strategically about his next move; he would need to lay the foundations in parliament first and get the approval he needed to wage a war against smuggling. Cecil's corrupt and ruthless mind quickly turned to the newly appointed Prime Minister William Pitt, the boy they'd sent to do a man's job, at only 24 years old he was the youngest to ever take the country's reins. Blackheath secretly detested the man with a passion, Pitt was young, naive and new in office; Blackheath would have no problems manipulating the younger man for the purposes of his own agenda, re-stealing his stone.

*

"The very next day Cecil Blackheath led a revolt in the Houses of Parliament to finally stamp out smuggling once and for all. He suggested leading a small army down to the worst smuggling town in the whole country, Deal in Kent, and setting an example that the trade would not be tolerated from this day forth. The smuggling trade had angered many of the old timers in the cabinet for decades and Blackheath used all his skills of manipulation to rouse support. Young William Pitt completely unaware of Blackheath's real intentions finally nodded his approval, giving Blackheath all the power he needed to bring Jacob Swift's empire to its knees. The greedy politician wasted no time; he desired the jewel more than anything in his whole life and knew that he needed to strike whilst the iron was still hot if he was going to stand any chance of getting it back. With the Prime Minister's approval

Blackheath gathered a small army and left London on the war path, arriving in Deal's cobbled streets the next day. The politician and his army caused quite a stir as they marched through the streets, people rushed out of their houses and the countless taverns to get a glimpse of the action. But it was what Blackheath did next that really caught everyone's attention and would be remembered in the pages of history books until the end of time.

"Leading his troops up to the shoreline that was littered with countless fishing vessels, essential to the town's livelihood, Blackheath ordered his men to douse them with paraffin and burn them all.

"'I don't want to see a single boat left seaworthy,' he barked at his troops, some of the locals tried to intervene but were beaten back with clubs, most just stood and stared in shock as the town's entire livelihood went up in flames. 'If I didn't have their attention when I arrived in the town, I certainly have it now,' he thought as he glanced at the crowd before stepping forward to address them.

"'My name is Cecil Blackheath and I'm here under the orders of the British Government! My task is to capture several thieves who dared to steal from a merchant ship anchored out in the downs,' he roared at the crowd before giving descriptions of the thieves to the men, women and children gathered who were now muttering amongst each other. 'I'm also here to locate and capture Jacob Swift, any information leading to his arrest will be rewarded handsomely,' he continued causing the crowd to become deadly silent and stare in shock, all but one, a tall man with a long ginger beard who was stood at the back of the crowd listening to Blackheath's speech turned around and quickly disappeared through the labyrinth of cobbled streets."

Chapter 40

"Jacob and Elizabeth Swift held hands and gazed into each other's eyes as their horse drawn cart with Thomas at the helm trotted along the Deal road past the Bay of St Margaret's. Leaning towards his new wife the undisputed king of smugglers kissed Elizabeth, the only woman he'd ever loved. It was a tender moment, a moment that, unknown to the happy couple, was destined to be their last.

"Suddenly the horses pulling the cart knead before skidding to an abrupt stop; instinctively Jacob pulled out a pistol from his waistband and held his wife tightly as voices were heard outside on the road. Leaning out of the carts small window Jacob spotted a dozen men on horseback, all heavily armed with rifles. The Boy's heart missed a beat but then his eyes fell on the man leading the gunmen. Alfie Bicks was recognisable a mile off with his ginger hair and beard blowing in the wind, but it was the grave look etched on his face as he trotted up alongside the cart that really caught The Boy's attention. Jacob Swift listened intently as his tall and trusted bodyguard explained about the devastating scene he'd witnessed down at the town's shore only an hour earlier.

"The Boy rubbed his temples and took a few deep breaths, he hadn't even reached the town's cobbled streets and already trouble had found him. Looking hard at Alfie, his close friend and a man that had watched his back since the first day he'd begun his smuggling career nearly a decade earlier, Jacob made a quick decision.

"'Arrange a crisis meeting immediately, get the entire back row to Bates' old headquarters as soon as possible,' he ordered, Alfie nodded and galloped off into the distance with half of his men whilst the other half stayed at their leader's side, escorting him safely to the old cliff-top house where Bates had taught him all the tricks of his trade.

"A short while later all the old faces began assembling in the study at Bill's old headquarters perched high up on the chalk cliffs overlooking The Channel. Every man that entered the study that day seemed more on edge than the last. Carp was the final man to arrive and take a seat before Jacob rose to his feet and the meeting began. The first topic of discussion was the apparent robbery on board the East India's merchant ship, an act that angered most of the men in the room.

"'Any idea who's responsible?' Jacob asked his gang who were scratching their beards and generally looking perplexed, all but one. It was Alfie Bicks who climbed out of his chair and towered over the table and the dozen men who were sat around it.

"'I'm pretty sure I know who robbed that ship, I heard on the grapevine that Eddie Biggs and his gang were in The Pelican a few nights ago, drunk as skunks and putting a fair bit of money behind the bar,' Alfie said, turning to his young boss. 'We haven't put any work their way for donkeys' years and, to be honest, I can't think of a better or more daring thief than old Eddie Biggs.'

"Every single man around the table was nodding his agreement as Alfie sat back down. Jacob was deep in thought contemplating Alfie's theory; The Boy knew Eddie Biggs well and knew the man was more than capable. Jacob couldn't afford to waste any time, he turned to Alfie. 'Alright I agree, take a few men and fetch Eddie and his crew.' The tall red-bearded bodyguard rose to his feet once more and slipped out of the study just as the conversation turned to the burning of the town's fishing fleet which roused up everybody's anger even more.

"'It's outrageous!' Hester stated. 'They've destroyed the town's livelihood. What are people going to do to survive?' Jacob's mathematician asked nobody in particular, but it was his young boss who answered

"'Times are going to be tough, there's no doubt about it but I'll do everything in my power to help this town's people,' he said before his mind began to drift, something didn't quite make sense and Jacob knew it even then. Cecil Blackheath's action was far too drastic, deep down Jacob knew the government were finally coming after him in an attempt to stamp out the smuggling trade once and for all; Eddie Biggs had sealed The Boy's fate and given the government a perfect excuse to wage war against him. 'Listen,' Jacob said, instantly silencing the dozen shady characters huddled around the table that Bill had taught him on a decade earlier. 'We may have to go underground again, but we have a dozen safe houses, a vast network of secret tunnels and thanks to our friend, Admiral Saunders, a constant supply of cash, in years past we've stuck together and overcome far greater obstacles than this.' Every man present was nodding their agreement with their young leader completely unaware of how wrong he was destined to be.

"Meanwhile, several miles away down on the shoreline Cecil Blackheath stood surrounded by soldiers watching smugly as the remnants of the town's fishing industry smouldered. Every now and again the crooked politician would glance over at the crowds and judging by the expressions on their faces Blackheath was confident he'd achieved his goal and captured Jacob Swift's attention.

"'I'm one step closer to getting the stone back,' he thought to himself as he watched a very smartly dressed rotund man stroll through the crowds towards him. Blackheath noted that the man didn't share that same look of devastation on his face like the others behind him; in fact he was actually smiling which made the crooked politician very curious. Finally when the man reached him he extended his hand which Blackheath shook.

"'I hear you've come for Jacob Swift,' the man asked, glancing left and right at the soldiers who flanked Blackheath on both sides.

"Blackheath nodded. 'Amongst other things' he replied as he watched the man in front of him smile with satisfaction.

"'That's good to hear,' he finally said. 'My name is Theodore Rawlings, the town's magistrate. I can supply you with all the information you require to locate Jacob Swift including most of the locations of his safe houses, I can also give you the name of one of the thieves that ransacked that ship, but I'm afraid I have one condition.'

"Cecil Blackheath stood rooted to the spot staring deep into the magistrate's eyes. 'And your condition?' he asked, to which Rawlings leant in close so that only Blackheath would hear.

"'Jacob Swift has to be taken out, not captured, There can be no trial,' Rawlings said, hoping with all his heart that the politician would agree. Theodore Rawlings didn't want to find himself locked up in the clink when The Boy finally spilled his beans about the corrupt magistrate and his illegal dealings. Blackheath smiled broadly as he nodded his agreement, he liked Theodore Rawlings already.

"Alfie Bicks marched along an old track, he was on edge constantly glancing over his shoulder on the lookout for soldiers, but, much to his relief, he didn't see a single soul. When he finally located the house where Eddie Biggs lived he breathed a sigh of relief, confident that Blackheath's men hadn't discovered the thief's identity yet. Alfie glanced at the door and for a fraction of a second he even considered knocking, in the end he felt better of it and instead he charged at it, smashing it off its hinges.

"Entering the shack he immediately came face to face with the business end of a musket held by Eddie himself, the man whose actions had unwittingly brought the entire town to its knees. Eddie gripped the weapon with a hand that shook uncontrollably, the thief tried standing his ground but then he recognised the scruffy red beard of his unexpected intruder and what little composure the man had mustered vanished, replaced by a look of absolute horror. Alfie remained completely calm and smiled, it wasn't the first time somebody had waved a gun in the tall bodyguard's face and it wouldn't be the last.

"'Eddie, it's alright, you can put the gun down I'm not going to hurt you. I've come to fetch you. Jacob Swift needs to talk with you,' Alfie said staring into Eddie's eyes, the thief was listening and at the mention of The Boy's name he finally lowered the musket.

"A short while later, Alfie Bicks strolled into Bates' old study with Eddie in tow, who was as pale as a sheet. The Boy was seated talking privately with Thomas, everybody else had left Bates' old headquarters to deal with the chaos erupting down in the town's cobbled streets. As soon as the pair entered the room, Jacob stopped the conversation he'd been having and ordered Eddie to sit, the thief took a seat in front of the young smuggler and began begging him for forgiveness.

"'I'm so sorry, we were desperate, Mr Swift,' he pleaded whilst Jacob stared at the pattern nature had selected on the mahogany table. 'We had no idea what was on board, it wasn't until we reached the shore that we realised and by then it was too late,' Eddie continued, Jacob's eyes shot up from the pattern on the wooden table and were now fixed on the thief in front of him.

"'What was on board? What do you mean?' he demanded. Eddie Biggs rummaged in his pocket for a moment that felt like a lifetime.

"'I've never seen anything like it,' he was mumbling. A moment later he pulled the item out of his pocket and placed it on the table, leaving Jacob Swift absolutely speechless. Alfie and Thomas had taken a step forward and were now crowded around the table. For a long moment nobody muttered a single word. The Eye of the Serpent, the biggest ruby the world had ever seen lay there on the mahogany table glistening as Jacob and his men stared in shock. At least a minute passed before anybody spoke. It was Alfie who eventually broke the silence

"'What the hell is that?' he asked.

"It was Eddie who replied, "I've read about it, it's a precious stone that was stolen from India month's ago. They call it the Eye of the Serpent.'

"'That's the reason the town's fishing fleet went up in flames earlier and the reason that politician Blackheath's in our town,' The Boy continued as he picked up the ruby in one hand. Jacob was surprised at its weight, but as he held the stone up to the light coming in from the window and watched as the jewel sparkled he was more surprised at its beauty.

"'That man Blackheath desperately wants this back and if we're to survive the next few days we need to cut a deal with him,' Jacob stated.

"It was Thomas who spoke next. 'Jacob this is a dangerous situation we've found ourselves in,' he warned, 'and I think we should get out of here immediately, this place isn't safe.' Jacob and Alfie both nodded their agreement. Jacob's most ruthless enforcer rarely spoke, but when he did you could guarantee it was for the most important of reasons. Thomas had lived on the town's dangerous streets as a child; he'd honed a survival instinct second to none.

"'If Blackheath's men catch us with the stone as well, we'll lose the only bargaining chip we have,' Jacob added, rubbing his chin for a moment as he racked his brain. A moment later he handed the large red jewel to Thomas who clutched the stone in his shovel-like hands.

"'Go and hide this, I don't want it put on any of our properties, put it where no one will ever think of looking. It has to be somewhere outdoors,' The Boy said before he smiled to himself. 'Actually I have just the place,' he glanced over at Eddie aware that the thief was listening to every word. Jacob beckoned the huge bodyguard over so that only he would hear the stone's hiding place when he whispered it into his ear. A moment later Thomas slipped the priceless ruby into his pocket and disappeared from the room. 'Let's go,' Jacob said nodding to Jim and Alfie who rose to their feet.

"'And what about me?' Eddie pleaded. 'What am I supposed to do now?'

"Jacob turned to face the thief that had landed him in a world of trouble. 'If I was you I would stay here, it has to be a lot safer than anywhere down in the town, there's food in the kitchen,' The Boy said using all his ability to remain calm and not show his true feelings. Jacob had his own reasons for keeping Eddie at the townhouse. The Boy figured that Eddie could be used as an extra bargaining chip with Blackheath if Jacob were to be captured by the politician. So Jacob Swift left Eddie Biggs in Bills old study, a move that was destined to be a huge mistake.

"Thomas had hidden the stone exactly where his young boss had suggested, it had been far from easy but the ruthless bodyguard had to admit it was somewhere that nobody would ever think of looking. Thomas was making his way towards the stables where he'd left his horse when he first sensed trouble, but by then it was way too late to do anything about it. Within moments he was surrounded by half a dozen soldiers on horseback who all held rifles levelled in his direction. Thomas feared nothing, but he wasn't stupid, he'd been raised by the great Billy Bates; the wise old rogue had taught him many things. Thomas knew when to admit defeat so he stood with his chin held high waiting for the gunshots that never came. After a few minutes a man appeared through the crowd that had gathered, he strolled towards Thomas with a huge grin etched all over his face. 'If he moves, kill him,' the man barked at the soldiers before turning to the bodyguard. 'I've waited a long time for this moment' Rawlings said as soldiers began shackling Thomas' legs.

"Eddie Biggs sat all alone in Bates' old study listening to the wind as it whistled over the English Channel and hit the windows making them rattle. The thief stared at the bookcases that were full to capacity and at the maps that covered the walls. Eddie had grown up in the town's dangerous streets and knew all about the great Billy Bates, the man was a legend and Eddie felt privileged to sit in the great man's study, the thief just wished it was under different circumstances.

"Eddie's thoughts were interrupted by a loud crash downstairs, the thief leapt to his feet in panic as a dozen boots trampled up the stairs. A moment later he was seated back down with half a dozen soldiers watching over him. At least a dozen more were ransacking Bill's old headquarters, smashing everything to bits and Eddie knew exactly what they were looking for. After a few minutes had passed a smartly dressed man strolled into the room, he glanced at Eddie and smiled as he pulled a dagger from its sheath hidden inside his jacket. Eddie knew the man was in charge even before he ordered the soldiers out of the study, leaving the pair alone. For a moment he simply smiled at Eddie, which terrified the thief who suddenly knew deep down in his guts that he had stolen from the man in front of him.

"'Eddie, I assume,' the man finally asked, to which Eddie simply nodded.

"'I'm Cecil Blackheath. Let's not waste any more of my time, agreed?' he said. Eddie nodded again as he glanced from the dagger in the man's hands and his eyes, quickly deciding that the man would have no problem using it.

"'Where is it?' Blackheath demanded, stepping closer towards the thief.

"'I don't have it anymore,' Eddie pleaded. 'Jacob Swift gave it to one of his men to hide.'

"For a moment Blackheath looked devastated, but a second later his expression turned to anger. 'Hide where?' he roared.

"Eddie flinched. 'I don't know, he whispered it so that I wouldn't hear, I swear to God.' Blackheath stared at the man in front of him for a long moment. 'I will do anything you ask,' the thief pleaded. Blackheath could tell that Eddie was not only terrified but also telling the truth, the politician took a deep breath and thought about the situation. He had to admit to himself that Jacob Swift was a very smart young man. Blackheath came to the conclusion that he respected his adversary before he finally spoke.

"'So which one of his men did he give the stone to?' he asked calmly in an attempt to put the thief's mind at ease. It worked and Eddie settled a little.

"'It was Thomas, he left to go and hide it, and then Jacob left. I think he wants to cut a deal with you,' the thief said, Blackheath smiled a wicked smile, the so called King of Smugglers rose in his opinion even more. Blackheath only cared about the stone and would do whatever it took to get it back. It didn't matter whether he cut a deal with The Boy or the magistrate he'd met earlier, Blackheath was loyal to no one.

"'So you don't know where the stone is?' Blackheath asked one last time.

"'I have no idea,' Eddie pleaded, the politician nodded smiling now. Just like his young adversary Cecil Blackheath was a master at hiding his true feelings.

"'And who else knows about the stone?' Blackheath asked, listening and making notes as the thief poured his heart out giving the names and addresses of his accomplices, men who'd helped carry out the robbery on board the merchant ship, men who Blackheath knew he'd have to silence just like the man in front of him. Finally once the thief had spilled his beans and the politician was confident he had heard everything he needed to hear Cecil Blackheath stepped forward and in one swift and savage move he buried the dagger deep into Eddie Bigg's right eye. For a moment the thief kicked and struggled as he tried to fight off death, but in the end it was a battle he was unable to win and finally his lifeless body fell forward slouching over the table where a puddle of blood began to collect on the mahogany surface. Blackheath retrieved his dagger and began cleaning the blade on Eddie's shirt. There was a knock on the study door. 'Come in,' he ordered just as a soldier appeared in the doorway. The man glanced at the grotesque scene in front of him and struggled not to look flustered.

"'A messenger has just arrived, the magistrate has captured one of Jacob's top men,' he said. Blackheath smiled as he replaced the dagger back in its sheath.

"'Which one?' he asked

"'The man's name is Thomas,' the soldier replied much to Blackheath's delight.

"When Blackheath left Bill's old headquarters he climbed into his carriage and was chauffeured down into the town's cobbled streets by a dozen heavily armed soldiers. During the journey all the politician could think about was his jewel; he believed with all his heart that he was close to getting it back. Blackheath believed that all he had to do was interrogate Thomas who would inevitably give up the stone's location under torture. Of course there were always the loose ends to tie up, people that needed to be silenced. The Eye of the Serpent and what Blackheath had done to get hold of it in the first place was his dirty secret and if it ever got out the politician would have a lot more than just his career to worry about. But, thankfully, according to the thief only a handful of people knew about the stone's existence. Blackheath was confident that he could still keep it under wraps.

"When he finally arrived down in the town he climbed out of his coach and was greeted by the magistrate, Theodore Rawlings, who informed him that Thomas, Jacob's right hand man and most feared enforcer of his smuggling empire, had been taken to the local barracks under armed guard, the magistrate looked extremely happy and Blackheath complimented the man on a job well done. As far as the crooked politician was concerned the magistrate had offered a deal and stuck to his side of the bargain, as soon as he had the stone in his possession Blackheath had no objection to sticking to his side and wiping Jacob Swift off the face of the earth. First though, Cecil Blackheath needed to make sure of one thing, he turned to Rawlings. 'This man Thomas,' he said, the magistrate nodded, 'I don't want a single hair harmed on his head, I need him alive, is that understood?'

"Rawlings nodded. 'Completely, as long as you don't leave this town until Jacob Swift is dead, that boy's been a thorn in my side for a very long time,' he said. Cecil Blackheath was just about to agree when the corrupt pairs' conversation was interrupted by a soldier who had galloped up to where they were stood; both men stared at the soldier whilst he caught his breath.

"'I bring news,' he finally managed. 'Jacob and several of his men were seen entering one of his safe houses on the outskirts of town, we have the place completely surrounded, he isn't going anywhere.'"

Chapter 41

"Jacob Swift sat on a barrel of rum surrounded by stacks of merchandise his men had smuggled into the country. Bales of tobacco filled shelves alongside great sacks of tea, whilst most of the floor space was filled with tubs of various liquors similar to the one The Boy was using as a seat. The building itself was an old stable surrounded by marshland. Jacob had been using it to store his goods for years, he'd chosen this particular safe house above the others partly because of its remote location, but mainly because few people knew of its existence.

"The Boy and his bodyguards had tethered their horses a few fields away in a small clearing surrounded by trees and made their way to the safe house along a dried-up ditch. As Jacob sat on the barrel all he could think about was his wife Elizabeth, during the couple's honeymoon they'd discussed their future and Jacob had confessed he was considering retirement. Sat in the dingy stable away from the woman he loved he made his decision, as soon as this trouble with Blackheath was over Jacob was giving up the smuggling trade once and for all. He planned on simply cashing in his wealth and disappearing. The Boy dreamed of climbing aboard one of his ships and sailing towards the horizon, where he wouldn't have to constantly look over his shoulder. One day, when he finally returned he would buy a farm out in the countryside far away from the town and the cobbled streets he'd ruled for over a decade.

"'Boss we've got company,' Alfie warned as he stood in the corner of the storeroom staring through a small crack in the brickwork. 'I can make out a few soldiers, they are crouching in the bushes several hundred yards away, my guess is they're waiting for backup.' Jacob turned to his old school friend Jim Robson who was just finishing loading a pair of pistols that he quickly tucked into his belt.

"'Let's go,' Jim said, as he searched for the handle of the hidden trapdoor in the stable's floor. A moment later he'd pulled it open and squeezed his huge frame through it, disappearing into one of the secret tunnel systems Jacob's men had dug out several years earlier, back when Jim had been wanted for Ronnie Jenkins rather brutal murder. Within moments Jacob followed, then Alfie who lowered the trapdoor back down slowly in the hope that it would buy the trio some more time to escape.

"Crawling through the filthy tunnel Jacob finally reached daylight on the muddy banks of the dried-up ditch. Jim Robson was already there peering over the bank at the stable a dozen or so metres away, and at the soldiers who were still crouched behind the bush waiting.

"'The coast is clear,' Jim whispered before the trio ran along the dried-up ditch towards where their horses were tethered.

"'How the hell did they learn about the safe house?' Alfie muttered as they made their escape.

"'I'm guessing they've already rounded some of our gang up,' Jim replied. Jacob remained silent; he no longer cared about his smuggling empire, the price of brandy on the continent or even priceless jewels from faraway countries. The only thing that mattered to Jacob now was his wife Elizabeth. He reminded himself that she was safe enough under the protection of her brother Michael and a handful of his most trusted men.

"Finally the trio reached the woodland where their horses were tethered, they were confident they'd managed to escape but then just as they ducked through the tree line out of sight the first of many gunshots filled the air.

"'Damn it,' Jacob muttered as he leapt onto his pure white horse and began galloping across the fields.

"Cecil Blackheath arrived at the safe house just in the nick of time to catch the country's most notorious smuggler making his retreat. It had been one of the soldiers under his command who'd spotted the smugglers disappearing into a patch of scrub in the distance. Moments later Blackheath and a dozen of his soldiers were galloping across the open fields of Kent, the Garden of England. Blackheath had the famous smuggler in his sights now and the crooked politician wasn't going to let him get away.

"Jacob, Alfie and Jim skirted around woodland and leapt over dikes at breakneck speed trying everything they could to shake off their pursuers, but nothing seemed to work. Finally Alfie tried the last thing he could think of, he pulled out a musket and opened fire on his pursuers in an attempt to slow them down. Blackheath's soldiers were determined though and they quickly returned fire, filling the air with a deafening roar of explosions.

"Jacob was charging ahead, he knew he was only a few miles away from Sandwich where several of his clippers were anchored on the River Stour. The Boy knew that if he could reach one of his vessels and make it out into The Channel then his chances of escape would be far greater than on land. He would sail over to the continent if need be, Jacob knew at least a dozen rich and powerful merchants over in France who would happily provide him with everything he needed. After all, these men relied on Jacob to make a living, like the hundreds across Kent who worked in the smuggling trade. 'But could I get as far as the docks to board a clipper?' he wondered before he glanced back at his pursuers noticing they were gaining with every gallop they took.

"'Swift! We need to split up,' Alfie shouted as he held onto his horse for dear life. 'Me and Jim will lead them off so you can reach the docks.' Jacob knew that if Blackheath's men caught Alfie and Jim the pair would be killed, he couldn't let that happen. Now that he was aware of what the politician was after he knew the man would stop at nothing to get it back. Jacob's bodyguards had risked their lives on countless occasions to save his skin, and in that moment The Boy knew the time had arrived to pay back the favour.

"'No! I will lead them away from you, it's me they're after,' Jacob shouted back over the thunder of hooves on the muddy track.

"'No! We won't leave you,' Jim Robson shouted back as a lone tear ran down his cheek. Jacob turned and stared into his friends eyes as the countryside raced past. The Boy had made his decision, deep down he believed he'd escape. Jacob had spent his life out on The Channel and knew the treacherous sandbanks better than anybody.

"'Listen, I'll be alright but if I'm not, just make sure Elizabeth is safe,' he shouted over the roar of hooves, as he stared at his friend who'd been teased about his weight many years ago and watched as tears streamed down his face, then Jacob turned to Alfie Bicks, the man who had watched his back and stood by his side since day one.

"'Thanks for everything,' Jacob said fighting off tears himself as a musket exploded behind him and a shot whistled through the air close by. 'Good luck', he said before pulling with all his might on his horse's reins and dramatically altering his course.

"'No!' he heard Jim scream before the pair disappeared behind some trees and Jacob galloped with all his might in a different direction.

"Cecil Blackheath and his soldiers didn't hesitate for a second when they saw the smugglers split up. The crooked politician was exhausted but he kept on Jacob's trail. Jim and Alfie were nobodies in comparison to the legend himself, Jacob Swift. Blackheath wasn't willing to take his eyes off the notorious smuggler who was clearly making a run for the docks. As they reached the outskirts of Sandwich the politician dug his heels in and mustered up what little energy he had left, determined not to let The Boy escape.

"Jacob galloped into the bustling docks. He didn't let up his horse's pace for a second, forcing people to jump out of his path for their dear lives. The Boy raced along the cobbled bank past a dozen merchant ships busy unloading a variety of exotic goods using all manner of winches and cranes. Jacob even spotted Admiral Saunders' man-of-war towering over the surrounding vessels; scores of its crew were busy on deck. Finally Jacob spotted several of his own clippers and a handful of his men preparing the ships for sail. Glancing back at his pursuers he was relieved to note the crowds had slowed their pace, but it was still way too close for comfort. Everything was happening so fast, as soon as Jacob was within earshot of his men he screamed the orders to raise anchor and drop sail. His men glanced up from their work recognising their young boss instantly, a fraction of a second later they were frantically carrying out his orders.

"Approaching at breakneck speed Jacob pulled with all his might to slow the horse before leaping from the animal and drawing two pistols which he levelled at the crowd. A split second later the first soldier appeared on horseback. Jacob fired a shot, deliberately missing the man by inches. The Boy glanced at his clipper in panic as his heart beat in his chest, its sails were raised and as it enjoyed the afternoon breeze the vessel began to drift away from the bank. Jacob Swift wasted no more time as he ran and leapt from the dock's landing on his ship's deck with a thud. Puffing and panting he raised his last pistol and aimed it at the docks but thankfully the first shot had produced the results he'd hoped for and slowed the soldier's pursuit.

"Jacob finally collapsed on his back and caught his breath as his clipper picked up speed and cruised out of the river's estuary and into the English Channel.

"When Blackheath reached the dock and climbed from his horse, he screamed in anger at the sight of the small ship sailing into the distance. The politician was used to getting his own way and despised being beaten. Blackheath had no intention of letting Jacob escape, not in his lifetime anyway. Feeling tired and frustrated, Blackheath took stock of his situation, and spotted the huge war ship that stuck out like a sore thumb around the small merchant vessels surrounding it. A moment later he was marching up the gangplank with a determined look etched on his face. 'I need to speak to the admiral of this vessel immediately,' he barked at one of the naval men who quickly disappeared below decks. The admiral appeared. 'Admiral Saunders' he said extending a hand which the politician shook.

"'Admiral I need to commandeer this ship on behalf of the British government,' Blackheath stated, the Admiral stared in shock at the politician and the dozen soldiers surrounding him.

"'May I ask why?' he replied.

"Cecil Blackheath wasted no more time, eager to finally catch Jacob. 'We need to apprehend this country's biggest smuggler,' he said causing the Admiral's heart to miss a beat. Saunders knew he had no choice but to comply with the politician's request.

"He turned to his first mate. 'Raise anchors and drop sail,' he ordered and within moments the huge ship had caught wind and was picking up speed.

"The Boy reached the mouth of the river and, as his clipper cruised out into the English Channel, Jacob believed he'd escaped. All he had to do was navigate through the treacherous sandbanks and cross over to France where he would be safe, but then he turned around once more and all his hopes faded. Jacob watched in horror as the huge seventy gun war ship came out of the rivers mouth in his clipper's wake. It had been a long time since he'd had to worry about the Navy, ever since he'd risked his life to save the Admiral's they'd posed no threat to his empire. Now he began to realise that escape might turn out to be more difficult than he'd previously thought. Turning his mind to Elizabeth and the rest of his gang, The Boy began to worry. The jewel was the only bargaining chip they had, and only he and Thomas knew of its location. In a frantic effort to get a message to the rest of his men Jacob rushed below deck and tore a piece of fabric from his shirt. For a split second he debated what to write, he couldn't give the exact location of the stone for fear of the message being intercepted so he scrawled a clue that only his men could translate before covering the fabric in candle wax and stuffing it into a bottle which he sealed with a thick cork and more wax.

"Scrambling back onto the deck, Jacob noted the warship had made progress and was now easily within firing range. He pulled out his telescope and scanned the horizon estimating his clipper to be only a few hundred metres away from the beginning of the sandbanks. The tide was high and Jacob knew his clipper would easily navigate over them where the warship would get grounded. Watching the sandbanks edge closer and closer, a little hope returned.

"Cecil Blackheath stared down at the small sailing ship that carried his prey and was confident the notorious smuggler had sealed his fate. He was pulled from his thoughts by one of his men. 'If he reaches the sands he'll slip through it, we'll have to navigate around them then we'll never catch him.'

"Blackheath scanned the horizon and considered his decision. The crooked politician didn't need Jacob Swift anymore, he had one of his men Thomas under lock and key and Blackheath was certain the man would give up the stone's location under torture. He figured that, either way, he needed to silence Jacob who knew of the stone's existence and he wanted to keep his promise to the magistrate too. Finally Blackheath turned to Admiral Saunders who was looking particularly troubled for a man who had earned a tough reputation for fighting battles at sea. 'Open fire and blow that ship out of the water,' he barked at Saunders who was now looking pale

"'But Sir,' the Admiral replied but was cut short.

"'That's an order, Admiral, and if you don't want to face the gallows for treason I'd carry it out immediately,' Blackheath roared. Admiral Saunders stepped back and glanced at the clipper; he owed Jacob Swift his life but was stuck between a rock and a hard place, leaving only one way out.

"'I'm sorry,' he muttered under his breath before turning to his second in command. 'Open fire,' he ordered through gritted teeth. Suddenly the warship shook as thirty-five cannons fired simultaneously launching a huge cloud of cannonballs down onto the small clipper, smashing her to pieces and sinking her in minutes. Blackheath watched the devastation unfold with a wicked smile on his face before turning to the Admiral and ordering the ship to return to the docks."

Chapter 42

When Reg stopped talking the silence in the museum quickly became unbearable. Stan sat staring at the floor trying to absorb the tragic ending to Jacob Swift's story. "So Blackheath had him killed just like that?" he finally mumbled. Reg smiled a sympathetic smile and nodded before he swallowed down the emotions brewing inside him. "But what about the ruby?" Stan asked, as Reg pushed his spectacles up the bridge of his nose.

"Cecil Blackheath knew that Thomas was aware of the stone's location. Blackheath was ruthless and had tortured countless men over the years. He believed he could obtain information out of anyone if they were given the right incentives," he said to Stan who was looking slightly pale. The story Reg had told him lacked the happy ever after he'd been expecting.

"And did Thomas give up the stone?" he asked eagerly, Reg smiled and slowly rose to his feet.

"Let's go get some fresh air." he said.

Stan was out of his chair in an instant. "I need to know," he countered.

Reg Cooper chuckled. "All in good time, lad, there's something I'd like you to see," he said.

With that the pair strolled out of the museum and locked it behind them. Reg put a notice on the door advising any potential customers that he'd gone fishing before they strolled across the road and into the graveyard of an old church. Reg hobbled along a narrow path past a row of headstones and sat down on a bench where Stan eventually joined him, then the old man continued the story he'd dedicated his life to.

Chapter 43

"When Admiral Saunders' ship returned to the port of Sandwich Cecil Blackheath departed thanking the Admiral and promising him that his loyalty wouldn't be forgotten. As the crooked politician strolled down the gangplank, Saunders struggled to keep his emotions in check. Ever since that storm in The Channel when The Boy had saved his life, he'd considered him a good friend. The Admiral would suffer for the rest of his life with Jacob's death on his conscience.

"Blackheath himself wasted no time returning to the town's cobbled streets and to the garrison where Thomas was being held. When the politician entered the dingy, cramped interrogation room, Thomas was already shackled to a chair much to Blackheath's relief. In the corner a soldier was stood heating up a poker on an open fire. Blackheath ordered the man to leave before turning his attention on the prisoner.

"'Thomas, isn't it?' he asked casually as he picked up the poker and admired its bright and glowing end. Thomas just stared at Blackheath prompting the politician to continue. 'I know that you know where my jewel is and that's all I want. This can either be painful, or painless, it really is your choice but either way you'll tell me what I want to know. Now where did you hide my stone?' he asked, approaching Thomas and holding the blazing poker just inches from his face.

"Thomas had a vacant look in his eyes, a look that Blackheath had never seen in all his years. Finally Jacob's most ruthless enforcer spoke, 'I made a promise to a great man many years ago that I would be loyal to Jacob Swift until the day I died,' he said, looking up from the floor and fixing his eyes on Blackheath's, 'and it's a promise I'd never break.'

"Cecil Blackheath stared at Thomas admiring the man's bravery, a quality he had great respect for. 'You'll tell me in the end, they always do,' he said stepping forward and pressing the red hot poker against Thomas' bare skin enjoying the screams of agony that followed."

Chapter 44

Reg Cooper stood from the bench pulling Stanley back to reality, the old curator hobbled over to a row of headstones, Stan followed debating whether or not to ask the question that was still nagging away at him, and finally he succumbed. "So did Thomas give up the stone's location?" he asked.

Reg had reached the row of headstones, he paused and turned to Stan. "Cecil Blackheath tortured Thomas for three days solid, and the man took more pain than Blackheath thought possible. As the hours ticked by the politician realised he'd made a huge error killing Jacob Swift so readily. On the third day, Thomas finally passed away leaving Blackheath in a fit of despair. The crooked politician had worked very hard obtaining the stone, it was the largest ruby the world had ever seen, a priceless treasure simply lost forever," Reg said before turning to face a gravestone.

Stan held back as his mind raced.

"In the end Blackheath ordered his troops to carry Thomas's tortured body down into the town's cobbled streets and dump it where everybody could see it as a message that smuggling would be tolerated no more," Reg said before turning to Stanley. "Of course Jacob's men took the body and gave it a proper burial here in this graveyard'. Stanley stood and approached the gravestone that Reg had been focused on. Reaching it, a knot twisted in his stomach and he stood speechless.

Thomas Bates
1753 – 1792

"It was only after his death that people realised Thomas didn't have a second name. Bill had been a father figure to Thomas so the name Bates seemed most appropriate," Reg said before the graveyard lapsed into silence.

A wave of depression washed over Stan as he realised that sometimes life could be just too unforgiving and cruel, his mind began to drift and, for the first time since meeting Reg, Stan thought of Daniel and the hell he'd been giving him at school for the past few weeks, now Stan's own problems seemed insignificant. Stan's mind raced with a thousand questions but he just didn't know where to start. "So where did Thomas hide the stone?"

Reg fixed him with a serious gaze. "I think they hid it at sea, just off the coast of Deal Castle in the same spot they'd anchored countless cargoes years before. Jacob didn't want it near any of his properties, it makes perfect sense," he said.

Stan thought about it. "It really is lost forever then," he said feeling more depressed than he'd ever felt.

Reg looked down at him through his spectacles and smiled. "Not all stories have happy endings I'm afraid, lad," he said as he rose to his feet and the pair began walking back to the museum in silence.

When they reached the museum, Reg began unlocking the door and as he struggled with the lock Stan's eyes fell on a bronze plaque above the museum's entrance. In the middle of the plaque was the curator's full name and, as Stan read it, his jaw went slack and he stood speechless. Reg opened the door. "Are you okay?" he asked glancing at Stan who was staring at him in shock.

The plaque simply read – 'Elizabeth Swift, owner and curator.'

Reg noticed what Stan had seen and smiled. "My mother's name was Elizabeth, she was named after her great-great grandmother," he said strolling into the museum.

Eventually Stan followed. "So..." was all he managed.

Reg turned to Stan. "Elizabeth was pregnant when Jacob was killed, she had conceived on her honeymoon. I'm the notorious Jacob Swift's only surviving descendent," he stated proudly.

Stan opened his mouth to speak but, "wow," was all he managed, his mind seemed so full of thoughts he struggled to contain them. Then suddenly something in his mind clicked and everything fell into place. Stan remembered what had brought him to the museum in the first place, the message from The Boy himself that had set Stan's weekend in motion.

He rummaged around in his bag whilst Reg stared at him curiously, then he pulled it out. He could hardly talk and Reg looked concerned. "I found this in an old bottle on the beach," he managed as he laid the message out on a table. Now it was Reg Cooper's turn to stand speechless as he stared in shock.

"Well I'll be damned," he muttered as he read the message several times. A moment later he rummaged in a drawer and pulled out an old battered journal, it was bound in leather and looked older than most of the museum's exhibits.

"What's that?" Stan asked as Reg compared the signature on the scrawled message with one in the old journal.

"This, my friend, is Jacob's journal, The Boy recorded everything in here; it's where I learnt most of The Boy's story and like half of the exhibits in this museum it's been in my family for a very long time," he said glancing up at Stanley. "This is Jacob Swift's signature all right and it confirms what I've believed all along, he hid the stone at sea, the line, 'Its hidden deep in the heart of my one true love', says it all. Jacob was born and bred on The Channel, it was his one true love."

Stan was feeling devastated. "So it really is lost then," he muttered, Reg noticed how depressed he looked and patted him on the back to cheer him up.

"I'm afraid so lad, it's lost out there in the sands forever," he said.

Stan sat staring at the odd exhibits as the minutes ticked past. He'd begun his weekend on an adventure and now it was all over he felt sad. He thought about what he'd learnt about the history of the town he came from and concluded that finding the message hadn't all been for nothing. He'd also met Reg Cooper and discovered how magical a place the museum could be, a place he knew he'd visit again. But, deep down, something was nagging at Stan, he couldn't quite put a finger on what that something was but he felt like Jacob Swift's story wasn't quite over yet. He climbed to his feet and strolled around the museum for a moment as the message flashed through his mind and the words 'buried deep in the heart of my one true love' repeated themselves in his mind. Stan reflected on how much he had in common with the notorious smuggler. Both had been raised by a single parent, both had been born into poverty. Jacob's life had been cut short at such a young age The Boy, like Stan, had his whole life ahead of him. He glanced at the tubs that many years before had been filled with brandy and smuggled back and forth on countless occasions, at the lamps smugglers had used to communicate with boats offshore, then his eyes fell on one of the exhibits and Stan was hit full force with the realisation that he knew where Jacob, The Boy, Swift had hidden the jewel.

Stan stood frozen to the spot for at least a minute whilst the truth sunk in, he couldn't be one-hundred percent sure but he was close enough; he turned to Reg Cooper who was seated at the entrance of the museum waiting hopefully for customers... like always.

"Buried deep in the heart of my one true love," he said aloud catching Reg's attention who stared at him looking puzzled, then Stan raised a finger and pointed at the figurehead carved from oak as a wedding present in 1792, the figurehead of Elizabeth Swan, Jacob Swift's one true love.

Reg Cooper's puzzled expression became more intense. "It can't be," he mumbled, but Stan was adamant.

"Think about it," he said. "On the wedding day the figurehead wasn't complete, that means your great, great grandmother Elizabeth received it after her honeymoon, after Jacob's death, after Thomas had hidden the stone."

Reg looked deep in thought for a moment as Stan leapt over a small railing and began trying to pull the figurine apart. Reg Cooper stood in shock for the briefest of moments.

"Stop Stan," he ordered. "That's been in my family for generations." But Stan wasn't listening, the young man was too focused on finding the seam where the wooden figurine had been joined.

A moment later he succeeded and with a sharp crack the two hundred year old figurehead began to split in two. Reg

Cooper was on his feet struggling towards Stanley in a futile effort to stop the boy destroying his family's heirloom. With a loud crack the whole figurehead came apart and both Stan and Reg stared at each other as silence filled the museum. Suddenly a creaking sound barely audible caught their attention and they both stared at the broken figurehead as The Eye of the Serpent, the world's largest natural ruby fell from its two-hundred year old hiding place and landed with a thud on the museum's floor.

Chapter 45

Reg Cooper's mouth fell open and his spectacles slipped down the bridge of his nose, the museum's curator failed to correct them and, along with young Stanley, he simply stared speechless at the priceless gem for a moment that lasted a lifetime. Finally, stepping on pieces of broken wood from the figurehead of his ancestor, Reg hobbled over and picked up The Eye of the Serpent as tears flowed down his cheeks. Reg Cooper reflected on the decades he'd spent searching for the stone, researching Jacob's story and hunting for clues to its location. In the end it had been with him all along. Reg glanced down at Stanley; the boy fate had brought to his museum, and ruffled his hair before handing Stan the huge ruby so he could grip the railing to stop him from collapsing with shock.

Stan looked up at Reg, a moment later he rushed over to the museum's doorway and grabbed a chair, he dragged it over and made Reg sit down so he could catch his breath. Then Stan turned his attention back to the stone, it was blood red and roughly the size of a cricket ball. He held it up towards the light and instantly understood why the stone had been worshipped. An expression Reg had used earlier came rushing back ... 'They believed they were the tears of gods'.

Suddenly Stan was dragged out of his thoughts by Reg who had wiped his eyes and regained a little composure. The old curator turned to the boy who had strolled into his museum. "Thank you Stanley from the bottom of my heart," he croaked. "Finding this stone was my biggest dream in life, the only dream I wanted to fulfil. My ancestor, Jacob Swift, was murdered and then labelled a thief, The Boy was many things but he never stole a thing in his entire life. All I've ever wanted was to clear his name. It's time the world knew the truth and not the story Blackheath used to cover his tracks," he continued as he picked up the telephone and began punching numbers.

A short time later a police car turned up at the museum and within a few hours the normally empty museum turned into a circus as the story broke and the world's media focused its attention on the tale of the notorious Jacob Swift, the King of Smugglers, a leader, husband and unknown to him... a father.

For weeks and weeks the story dominated the tabloids as the town and its shady smuggling history was put in the spotlight. The truth about the country's youngest and most notorious smuggler finally came out, much to Reg Cooper's pleasure who'd struggled for a lifetime trying to clear his family's name.

Both Reg and Stan became local celebrities; they both played an important role in the story, like Thomas or even the old rogue Bill Bates himself. As the story circled the globe Stanley became a hero, not only in the town's cobbled streets but also in the school playground.

Stan found that suddenly everybody wanted to be his friend, Daniel Ryan and the other bullies included. The museum became an overnight success, Reg found that not only was it full to capacity but there was often a queue outside. The old curator relished sharing the town's history, he was happiest when re-telling the story to eager visitors.

As far as Reg Cooper was concerned, the ruby didn't belong to him, it never had. It belonged to India and its people. The old curator donated the stone free of charge to the National Museum of India in New Delhi so that the stone would always remain in the country where it belonged. The museum's initial reaction to Reg's generosity was shock, they considered it an incredibly honourable gesture and the curator in India in return allowed Reg Cooper and his small maritime museum full access to over half a million exhibits. Several weeks later Reg was contacted by an Indian businessman who had been so impressed he anonymously donated an immense sum of money to Reg's museum, most of which Reg put into a trust fund guaranteeing the museum would stay open for a long time after Reg was gone and the people of Deal would never forget their roots. Reg also set aside some money for another cause. The old curator owed everything to the young man who had strolled into his museum asking questions about his ancestor. Stan and his mother moved out of the tiny flat above the newsagents which had been one of the things Daniel and his gang had bullied him about; they moved into a nice house with a big garden where Stan could play football.

Reg Cooper himself had no family, the old curator knew that one day he would need to find a successor, but as you can guess he had his eyes on someone already.

Chapter 46

A few months later...

Stanley stood in the graveyard staring at Thomas's grave. Out of all the characters in The Boy's story Thomas had been his favourite. Stan couldn't even imagine the pain Jacob's bodyguard had endured when Blackheath had tortured him, and he'd been loyal to his boss until the very end. Stan had come to learn that loyalty was a trait he really respected in people. Thinking about some of the other characters, Stan realised that he hadn't found out what happened to them in the end. Finding the stone had been such a huge distraction he hadn't even thought about it until now.

He stepped forward and placed some flowers on the grave before strolling out of the churchyard and towards the museum. Like always since they had found the stone, the museum was busy.

When Stan entered Reg Cooper's face lit up and he rushed over from where he had been re-telling the story to some visitors. A moment later Stan was recognised and for the next ten minutes he found himself having his photo taken. A short while after the guests left Reg hobbled over and took a seat next to Stan. "So lad, how are you?" he asked, puzzled by the look on young Stan's face.

"I'm curious about something actually," Stan replied causing the old curator to laugh whole-heartedly.

"When aren't you lad?" he asked. "What's on your mind?"

"Well you never got round to telling me what happened to Alfie Bicks or Jim Robson," Stan said. Reg Cooper chuckled. "Well that's a very good question, and I hope you've got some time on your hands because that's a whole new story," he said as Stanley's face lit up. Reg smiled and pushed his spectacles up the bridge of his nose.

TO BE CONTINUED...